HE'S SO NOT MY VALENTINE

A SMALL-TOWN, SINGLE-MOM, RELUCTANT TO FALL ROMCOM

SAVANNAH SCOTT

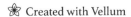 Created with Vellum

CONNECT WITH SAVANNAH SCOTT

You can connect with Savannah at her website
https://SavannahScottBooks.com/

You can also follow Savannah on Amazon.

For free books and first notice of new releases,
sign up for Savannah's Romcom Readers email

For Jon
You and me.
Highs and lows.
Through the years.
Choosing us over and over.

For all those reluctant romantics.
For the people who think their chance has passed them by.
For the guarded hearts.
May you find your valentine.
And may he love you well.

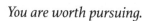

You are worth pursuing.

*Find the love who would travel an ocean for you,
the love that will outlast the hard days
and cherish all the moments in between.*

1

RENE

It's fine. I'm fine. Everything's fine.

~ David Schwimmer (Ross in Friends)

I toss my keys in the bowl by the door, slip my shoes off and walk into my flat. My ears still ring with the dull thump of the bass beat at the dance club, making the usual silence of my apartment feel less poignant. Still, there's no denying I live alone. The consummate bachelor, that's what Pierre calls me. He's half-teasing, sure. And, he's not wrong. I'm in my early thirties, yet still living the lifestyle he and I shared in our twenties.

Before he met Tasha.

Before he took off for America.

Before he fell in love and decided to defect.

How any man could trade France for the states is beyond me. So, he fell in love. Women move here all the time for love. She could have come here and fallen in love with

France. What's not to love? I'm truly happy for Pierre and Tasha. I just ... miss him. We have been inseparable since boyhood. And now we're an ocean apart.

I grab a glass and fill it with water. All that dancing and the few drinks I had earlier tonight will catch up with me tomorrow if I don't rehydrate before bedtime.

The bass of the song from the club seems suddenly louder.

No. That is not the residual sounds of the club still echoing in my head. That is my neighbor.

I hear voices. Giggling, loud voices. "Oui, Jean Claude. Oh, but I shouldn't." They may as well be in my kitchen.

"No. She shouldn't." I quip to no one but myself.

"Ahhh. Stop, Jean Claude!" comes my neighbor's sing-song voice through the paper-thin walls. I pay plenty for this property near the downtown of Avignon. It's an historic building, built in an era where, so it seems, privacy was not a top priority. Or even a consideration, apparently.

"Please stop, Jean Claude," I mutter to no one in particular.

I need a dog. Or a cat. Or earplugs. Maybe a dog and a cat and earplugs.

A loud, playful squeal followed by peals of laughter filter through the wall next. What are they even doing? Playing hide and seek? Having a pillow fight? I feel like a voyeur, but I'm not asking for this side-show at ... what is it? It must be at least half past midnight. No. I take a second look. Oh. It's two ten in the morning. How did I not realize it was this late?

"Go to sleep, Jean Claude. Or home. Even better. Go home." I don't speak loudly in case he might actually hear me. Obviously, the lack of soundproofing goes both ways.

"Léna," a man's voice rumbles. Must be Jean Claude.

Oh yes. That was her name. I had forgotten. Well, thanks, Jean Claude. You saved me from that awkward moment when I would run into Léna on the street or at the postal boxes and she greets me while I shift nervously trying to recall her name.

"Léna, oh, cher."

Okayyy. Time to ... go to bed. That's what I'll do. I grab my cell from my pocket, while I walk toward my bedroom, which thankfully does not share a wall with Léna's apartment. No, my bedroom overlooks the courtyard and gardens. I have a small balcony. Double doors lead out there, but I've never stepped foot on it. I love adventure, but testing centuries-old architecture and gambling as to whether it could hold my body weight would be a stretch—even for me.

I unbutton my shirt as I walk across the living area to my private quarters, a simple bedroom with an adjoining bath. On what feels like a whim, I push the button to call my best friend. The moment I hear the ring, something in me settles.

"Allo?" Pierre's friendly greeting brings a smile to my face.

The neighbors' voices are mere mumbles now. I shut my bedroom door and recline onto my bed.

"Allo, mon ami. Comment vas-tu?" I settle into the pillows along my headboard, setting my phone on one and pushing the speaker button.

"Rene! What has you calling at this hour?"

"A man can't call his best friend?"

"You can, of course. It's just late evening here. ... Wait! It's two eighteen in the morning there. What is wrong?"

"Nothing. Nothing. I can't sleep. So I thought, Pierre is awake. Am I right?"

"You are."

"Is that Rene?" I hear my best friend's American wife say in the background.

"Oui," Pierre answers her.

It does my heart good to hear Pierre speak in French to Tasha. I feared he would abandon everything about our country once he decided to remain in America with her.

"Put him on speaker," Tasha says, her voice near enough to the phone now. She's probably snuggled on the couch with Pierre. I'm not jealous. I'm happy for him. He's the last man I thought would settle down. Not that he's not suited for stability and family life. He's definitely long-term commitment material and a one-woman man. He was just so badly burned by his last relationship, I never imagined him finding what he has with Tasha. And I'm glad. Really. I am.

They both deserve to be deliriously happy.

Not everyone is meant to couple up as if they are animals pairing to walk the gangway into Noah's Ark. Some of us are meant to roam and remain free agents. And, by some of us, I mean me.

I glance around my flat in historic Avignon. The restored 1400s building has charm and elegance to spare. I've worked hard to establish myself as an agent immobilier, or what they call a real estate agent in the states. I'm happy. I have friends, family, and an excellent career. I travel when I like. I leave my dishes in the sink if I'm feeling wild and crazy. If I want companionship, I go out dancing or into town, or I ask a woman out for an evening.

Whenever people ask me if I want to settle down, I tell them, *probably*. That's my polished and practiced answer. I say, in as general a way as possible, something like, *What man wouldn't want a wife and a bunch of cute children?* I'm not lying, just giving the answer that has spared me being set up with everyone's niece, coworker, and that one woman who just can't seem to find Mr. Right. Only, it turns out there's an army of this type of woman. And I've dated her and all her friends.

I'm a marvelous date. Not to brag, but I have all the manners. I've honed my ability to genuinely attend to a woman like a craftsman masters his trade. I am romantic, charming, and I always make a woman feel like she is special —because every woman is. But, alas, I feel nothing. I don't feel compelled to settle down—or at least I haven't so far in my over thirty years of life. Not one woman I've dated makes me wish she'd leave the toothpaste open next to my sink, or that I'd wake to her morning after morning to share a cup of coffee and the kind of conversation only people who spend a lifetime together experience.

The interior silence of my apartment suddenly taunts me. But it is late. Of course it is quiet and still. I can't hear my neighbor anymore. No one is up flushing my toilet, or rolling over to drape her arm over me, or snoring loudly to interrupt my peaceful night's sleep. Aside from the noise that occasionally filters in from next door, I am alone. It is good. I come and go as I please.

"Rene, are you still there?" I hear Tasha's voice, and then I see the video icon light on my screen.

"Yes. I'm here."

I push to accept their video chat, and as I expected, they are on the couch, Pierre's arm casually perched behind Tasha, wrapping around her and pulling her near as they smile into the phone at me. Pierre's other hand rests comfortably on his wife's abdomen, over the place where she's carrying their child. She's four and a half months pregnant with their first baby, and they still refuse to put me out of my misery by finding out the gender.

"Oh, good! Video chats are so much more fun, don't you think?" Tasha asks.

I hold the phone toward my face as I climb out of bed, walk to my closet, and take off my shirt to throw in the hamper. I set the phone on a small shelf in my closet and pull an undershirt over my head. I leave the phone aimed at my ceiling while I slip out of my pants and into pajama bottoms.

"A little warning would be nice," I joke as I pick the phone up again, walk back to bed and prop it on the side table, climbing into bed so I can chat comfortably with two of my favorite people in the world.

"Same here," Pierre says. "I'm not sure I needed my wife to see your bare chest. I don't do pushups every morning like you do. It's unfair for her to have the comparison."

He's smiling, and I chuckle.

Tasha turns to Pierre. "I didn't even notice." And then she kisses him on the cheek.

Pierre's smile is wide.

Tashsa leans in toward the screen of the phone. Her brows are drawn up slightly with an expression of either concern or pity. "What have you been up to? And why can't you sleep? Is everything okay?"

Pierre kisses Tasha's temple. "One question at a time, Cher. He needs a chance to answer you."

She smiles up at him.

They've been together for nearly a year and a half now, and their love seems only to be growing stronger with time.

A feeling I can't name overwhelms me. Longing? Jealousy? It's as if something's missing and I can't find it. I push all that aside. It's late. I need sleep. Mornings always feel better. Middle-of-the-night crises shrink back to right-sized annoyances in the light of dawn.

"I've been out to a club dancing tonight. Pierre knows the one. When you come to Avignon again someday, we'll take you out and show you everything. There's more to our city than his family's home and the surrounding Provence region."

"I hope we get to take you up on that sometime," Tasha's eyes nearly sparkle.

"Of course you do. France is magnifique."

She smiles at me, then pats her belly. "It might not be for a year or so. I want to take the baby when we go, but I want to make the trip easy. So, maybe a year from now?" She looks up at Pierre, who merely nods.

"A year." My voice sounds flat, even to my own ears.

I'm like a child waiting for Christmas. Will I really have to wait a year to see these two face-to-face?

"You could always come here," Pierre offers. "Your business is flexible. You have no wife and children to consider."

Thanks for reminding me.

"Come there?"

"Oui. Come. We have a room. It will be the nursery soon, but for now it has the bed you stayed in last time. Come to North Carolina, Rene."

"Oh! You have to come!" Tasha nearly bounces in her seat. "We'd love to see you."

Pierre is correct. My life here is flexible. I have colleagues who can do showings. Many clients prefer to view homes via my video tours which I now outsource to a videographer I've known for years. I can finalize deals from anywhere. Other agents in my office could cover any in-person work if I took a holiday.

"Maybe I will come."

"Please do." Pierre's face is sincere. "I miss you."

"Ahh. I miss you too. Okay. Let me see what I can work out. I'll let you know."

Tasha leans her head onto Pierre's shoulder and yawns.

"I'm sorry. This baby makes me so sleepy. I think I'll head to bed. Sorry to be a party pooper."

"A what?" I chuckle.

She laughs softly. "I'm sorry for cutting our conversation short. We call that being a party pooper."

"America." I shake my head.

"Right?" Tasha smiles and shrugs. "Well, goodnight, Rene. Let us know when you can come. The room is just sitting here empty, waiting for you. I have friends who would love to spend time with a Frenchman. We'll make sure you have fun while you're here. It's actually really good timing. Pierre just published a book. He's starting the next one, but we're in a lull."

"Okay," I assure her. "I'll make plans."

"Good," Pierre says with a nod of finality. "We look forward to seeing you."

2

HEATHER

Love is in the air ... but so is the flu.

~ Unknown

"What's all this?" Tasha asks, when she walks through the door of Cataloochee Coffee.

"I'm decorating for Valentine's Day." I step off the ladder I have pulled up against the front plate-glass window and stand back to admire the garland of pink, white, and red felt hearts interspersed with pom-poms I just hung there.

"I thought you hated Valentine's Day," my sister says with almost a note of accusation in her voice.

She's the romantic in the family. I'm more of the practical one. A realist. And it wasn't the fact that my ex, Andrew, cheated on me and left me to raise our amazing son single-handedly that turned me into a pessimist when it comes to all things romance. I've always had a healthy dose of skepticism when it comes to the dreamy side of life. While Tasha has always thrown herself headlong into all things lovey-dovey, I tend to keep my feet on the ground. Sure, I'll admit the initial rush of new love brings all sorts of heady feelings and pie-in-the-sky thoughts. That stage is only infatuation, really. It boils down to a chemical response, triggered by pheromones and other stimuli. Eventually, that euphoria wears off. And what are you left with? Reality. A man who stinks when he comes home from a run. A man who can't bother to remember your birthday. A man who watches TV instead of engaging in conversation.

Dating can be sweet, even intoxicating. Though, you won't find me dating anytime soon. I've got no free time, and if I did, it would be spent on a hike in the Blue Ridge Mountains, or hanging out with my eight-year-old. But dating isn't the problem. It's the long haul that does a couple in. Over time, a relationship loses all its charm and marriage ends up sadly resembling trying to get a toddler to take a nap, only insert a grown man into that scenario. No thanks.

And celebrating a day named after a man most people know very little about? I don't know. It's a bit far-fetched. Saint Valentine is the patron saint of lovers, epileptics and beekeepers. All dangerous things. None of which seem worthy of celebration every year with chocolates and roses and platitudes that are easily tossed off the following week like a bouquet of wilted flowers.

"I'm not a fan of the day, true," I admit. "But my customers love it. So ... I'm obliging them by putting up some decorations and making a few themed treats. Emmy is baking some mini strawberry tarts in little heart shaped tins and I'll have those out next week in the display case."

"Well, good for you, stepping past your utter hatred for the holiday to bless your customers."

"They aren't officially *my* customers. Stan and Melanie still own this shop. For now."

Speaking of my eight-year-old, the door swings open and he barges in with his usual commanding presence. He's always been like that: loud, bold, funny—the opposite of me. And I adore every raucous inch of him.

"Hey, Aunt Tasha! Whatcha talkin' about? Hi, Mommy. Can I have a cookie?"

"After homework. I left you some carrots and hummus in the back fridge."

Nate scrunches up his nose.

"We were just talking about Valentine's day and how your mom's not the biggest fan of that wonderful day," Tasha tells Nate with a wink.

Ever the younger sister. She and Nate team up on me more often than not.

"I hate it too," my son declares. His face scrunches up even more than when I offered him a healthy snack. "All the girls go coo-coo asking to be my valentine."

"Do they?" Tasha's eager grin takes over her face.

Nate's gaze flicks to mine. "Chill out, Mommy. I'm not getting a valentine. Even if she gives me her chocolate milk at lunch. I'm not even seventeen."

His logic always entertains me.

"Seventeen, huh?" Tasha asks Nate. "What's so special about being seventeen? Why not eighteen or twenty?"

Nate scoots his backpack off his shoulder and plops it on the floor next to the couch I have at the front of the shop. I give him a mom-look and he picks it back up. This place may feel like home to him, but it's a business. He knows to put his belongings in the office when he comes here after school.

Nate smiles at Tasha and wiggles his eyebrows. It's a move that takes my breath away. He's going to be seventeen in a blink, and then I'll have so much more to worry about. Raising him without a man in his life now is fine. When he's a teen boy, I'm pretty sure I'll be in over my head.

Nate's voice is full of confidence. " 'Cause if I'm seventeen, I'll have a six pack and a car. Then I can kiss a girl. Unless she's gross. Jackson's seventeen. He thinks kissing is fun."

What? What? What? A six pack? A car? Well, I guess he will have a car. But a six pack? And kissing? I plop onto the couch. Tasha looks over at me and chuckles.

"Jackson told you that?" I ask. I'm going to have a talk with one seventeen-year-old, and pronto.

"No." Nate's eye roll is dramatic. "Jackson was kissing Stacey Hargraves outside—right there. Like this."

Nate points to the sidewalk, right in front of the shop. Then he puckers up and dramatically moves his face about like he's trying to untwist a bottle with his lips. He's not finished with his demonstration, either.

"Jackson was all ..." My son puts his hands in the air like he's holding someone's head, then he puckers again and keeps moving his head around with his eyes closed. "Then he smiled really big when they stopped kissing. Like I smile when you say we're getting pizza." Nate makes a face like I forced him to eat spinach. "Just gross."

He looks out toward the spot where Jackson and Stacey were kissing. "Probably by the time I'm seventeen, I might actually smile about kissing girls too."

I shake my head and look at my sister who is obviously

holding back laughter for my sake. She has this devilish grin and she's obviously biting the inside of her cheek.

"I gotta do my homework," Nate announces, abruptly changing the subject as boys his age are prone to do. He starts to peel his jacket off with one hand while he walks toward the back of the store, carrying his backpack in the other.

Once he's out of earshot, Tasha lets her laugh out and then she says, "Man, oh man. Are we in trouble with him, or what?"

"Tell me about it."

Tasha and I walk to the front of the shop. I stop at a few tables along the way, checking if customers need anything and clearing empty cups and plates as I go.

"Hi, Mrs. Smart," I greet one of my regulars. "Can I get you anything else?"

"Jeannie, Heather. It's Jeannie. It's been years since you girls were in high school. I keep telling you to call me by my first name."

"I know. I know. One day I just might."

She smiles warmly at me.

"I'd love a cherry scone to go. I'm going to surprise Emmy and stop in at Book Smart with a little treat for her."

"Aww. That's the sweetest. I'll be right back with that."

I hand Tasha the stack of saucers and cups while I head to the display case to pull out the best scone I can find and plop it into one of the paper bags I keep for to-go orders. Tasha walks into the kitchen to drop off the dirty dishes.

"Oh! Guess what?" she says when she emerges from the back of the shop.

"What?"

"Rene might come visit us for a while."

"Rene, Pierre's friend? That shameless flirt of a man?"

"That's the one. You remember him. And, I've told you. He's not as bad as he seems. He's harmless. He actually lives a pretty quiet life in Avignon."

"Yeah. I bet he does. He seems like his life is nothing but dull."

Rene seems like he's one of those guys who has a little black book full of names of women lining up for a chance at even one night out with him. He's got that whole European allure going for him too. Not that I'd know. My life has been spent in the same hundred-mile radius. I've never even traveled outside of North Carolina. Then again, if a woman's going to live her entire life somewhere, she could do far worse than Harvest Hollow and the surrounding towns.

But that Rene? He's definitely been around the world. And he knows how to look a woman in the eyes with a piercing glance that could make her weak in the knees. Not me, obviously. My knees are fortified and in no danger from men like him.

Tasha shakes her head at me. I know she wishes I would soften up and make room for men in my life.

I wipe the counter while reminding myself I've got nine years until my son turns seventeen. No one's kissing anyone this Valentine's Day. At least no one in my immediate family.

3

RENE

After a fourteen-hour travel day yesterday, I wake in Pierre's guest bedroom. I fell asleep embarrassingly early. And I woke to pitch blackness outside, but forced myself to go back to sleep. Now the sun is up and noises are filtering into my room from the kitchen. My stomach growls, reminding me I skipped breakfast—in France we'd be nearing lunchtime by now. I rouse myself and get dressed.

"Coffee?" Pierre asks when I pull out a chair at the dinette table—this same table where I sat over a year ago, laying out rules for his contrived marriage to his now wife. Ah, how the mighty fall.

"What's so amusing?" he asks me, in French.

"Nothing. I'm thinking of the rules we wrote and how you two blew through those with such blatant disregard."

He smiles widely. "You know you set those up just to watch us break them."

I raise both hands in a show of innocence. "Moi? No. I was looking out for you."

I wink, and Pierre smiles the smile of a man extremely content with his life. He places a filled cup in front of me. The coffee is black and thick, the way I like it. Strong and pungent. I take a sip.

"What about pastry?" I ask.

"For that, you will need to go into town."

"Ah. To the shop Tasha's sister runs?"

"They have the best."

"We have the best," I remind him.

"Oui. I won't argue that. There are no croissants in America as good as those back home."

"You could live anywhere."

"And I happily live here."

"Mmm." I hum into my cup.

You can't blame a man for trying to woo his friend back to his homeland. And there's nothing like a French croissant to do the job.

Tasha joins us, leaning down and placing a kiss on her husband's cheek. He swivels and captures her mouth in a kiss on her lips. I turn my head and look out the back windows into the woods off their deck. The trees are bare and crisp, unlike the fall when I was last here and the scenery was a mass of reds, yellows, oranges and burgundies. Still, there's a wisp of promise in the wintery view—the knowledge that these branches will fill with life again in a few months, bright greens dotting the now barren twigs.

I smile at the thought.

Tasha stands behind Pierre, wrapping her arms around his shoulders. He leans back into her embrace. It's a sight to see my formerly very-single friend so comfortable in his marriage. It suits him. Still, it takes some adjusting on my part. I had always been the one dating and surrounding myself with female friends and casual romantic involvements. Pierre was more of a serial monogamist, and then he had one relationship that I thought ruined him for ever trying again. But, here he is, like the woods behind his house, full of life where he appeared to have no hope of anything other than solitude.

"I thought we'd take a trip into town," Tasha suggests. "Maybe we could grab some pastries at Cataloochee Coffee?"

"Were you eavesdropping?"

"No. Why?"

"I just asked for a pastry with this coffee."

"That is not coffee," Tasha teases. "It's motor oil."

Pierre chuckles. "She has learned French, but she will never love our coffee."

"Comme c'est tragique," I say, shaking my head.

"My distaste for bitter coffee is not a tragedy," Tasha says with a warm smile. "But, drinking that without a pastry, well, that might be."

"I don't need any more convincing. Let's go into town."

Pierre and I rinse our cups and the three of us take the short drive into town, out through his sprawling, wooded neighborhood where the homes are set apart on winding streets, down a hill, past a lake, and then into more compact neighborhoods where the houses sit tucked closely together, and finally, onto a street that runs through the quaint downtown district of Harvest Hollow. The buildings are mostly brick and stone, some of the shops have awnings. It's like a scene from an American movie. The lampposts have banners with hearts on them and every other banner bears some cliché saying about love.

"Ah, it is coming near to the holiday of Saint Valentine, isn't it?"

"Yes," Tasha answers me from the front passenger seat. Then she turns to Pierre. "Heather even decorated the shop. I was impressed."

"Does she not usually decorate well?" I ask.

Tasha turns so she can look at me through the space between the two front seats. "My sister is not a fan of Valentine's Day. But she's always doing things to add a special touch for her customers."

"It is a silly day," I say, thoughtlessly.

"It's not!" Tasha says. She's smiling at me, but her eyes tell me she's ready to defend this holiday if need be.

"A day when you force men to attend to the women they love?" I ask. "Should they not be doing that every day? Why have a holiday to make a show of it?"

"Exactly," Pierre agrees. Then he looks over at Tasha and begins to pedal in reverse. "Though, it's wonderful to celebrate with you. I love the extra reminder. It's ... my favorite. J'adore le jour de la Saint-Valentin."

He loves Saint Valentine's Day? I almost call him out. But when I see the smile on Tasha's face, I drop it.

Then, I can't help myself.

"Yes. Back home, we even nicknamed your husband Saint Valentine. Pierre Valentine, we all called him."

"You did not!" Tasha laughs through her words.

"Okay, we did not. Not at all. But you have made him a convert. That much is evident."

She beams back at me, proud of her influence, as she should be. Every man should be so lucky.

We park in one of the spots on the street in front of the coffee shop. I pull my scarf close around my neck when I exit the car. The weather here is much like Avignon. Brisk in the winter, but not deadly cold. A bell over the shop door jingles as we step inside. I'm immediately surrounded by warmth. The air feels cozy and inviting, The smells of coffee, chocolate and spices draw out an involuntary sigh.

And then I see her—Heather, Tasha's sister. She's standing near a table, laughing at something one of two older gentlemen just said. Her hand is on her hip, a half-apron covering the front of her jeans. Her white T-shirt should seem plain, but it only serves to accentuate her understated beauty. Where Tasha has curly auburn hair, Heather's is more of an almond color with blonde highlights so prevalent she looks like a blond one moment and a brunette the next. She's wearing it at a length that falls to just beyond her shoulders these days. Heather's a classic beauty, and obviously a woman unaware of her own allure.

She puts her hand on the shoulder of one of the men at the table and says something that brings smiles to both their faces. Then she moves on to another table, asking a question, picking up a used cup and saucer. She continues moving further into the room, pausing, talking, cleaning. I watch her smile and listen to people as she makes her way to the back where a swinging door leads into what I assume is the kitchen area.

Pierre and Tasha find an empty table in the middle of the

room and Pierre helps Tasha out of her coat. I go through the motions of removing my own coat and scarf and draping them over the extra chair while my eyes follow Heather. She's back out from the kitchen, refilling cups from a carafe she's carrying, then speaking with authority to one of her employees. He runs off to get something from behind the counter. Heather doesn't sit still, but moves from spot to spot like the consummate hostess at a party, attending to each person before moving to the next. When she looks our way, a smile blooms across her face. Heather's looking at her sister. And then her eyes meet mine and the smile morphs into something slightly more guarded.

She approaches our table.

"You remember Rene," Tasha says to Heather.

Her eyes drift over toward mine. "Oh, yes. Who could forget?"

Ah. So, I made an impression. That tone, though. It lights a fire in me. I remember Heather too—a woman completely unimpressed with me. Her ability to verbally spar belies the way she deals so gently and graciously with all her customers and her family.

It would seem that I rub her the wrong way. Why? I don't know.

I look into Heather's brown eyes. They are focused and warm. I study the flecks of gold scattered in the deeper brown like stars in a night sky or bits of caramel in a brownie. She's staring at me with barely-veiled intensity. It's like she's daring me to win her over. Not that I'm trying to win anyone. I'm only here in the states for three weeks. But I am a man who loves a challenge. And the way Heather's staring at me, her mouth slightly pursed, her brow cocked, her eyes unflinching, suddenly makes me feel alive in places that seem to have been numb for some time now.

"So, I'm unforgettable?" My voice is teasing.

I wag my eyebrows as I stand to greet Heather in the traditional French way with a faire la bise. It's a light kiss to both cheeks. I'm well aware they do not greet one another this way in America. I'm also aware that Heather would rather I keep my faire la bise to myself. But something tells me she also wants my kisses to her cheeks, so I walk over as nonchalantly as possible, drawn to her, despite my better judgment.

I come around the table and Heather's posture grows increasingly rigid as I approach her. Her arms cross, but she's still looking me in the eyes. She knows what I'm doing. After all, Tasha's in-laws have all been here several times to visit since Pierre moved here. And I have been twice as well. This is actually my third trip to the United States. The things I do for my friend.

I grasp Heather's shoulders lightly and quickly kiss each of her cheeks. She's stiff, but she doesn't pull away. "So good to see you again," I say. "You are looking beautiful this morning."

"Mm hmm," she mumbles as she pulls back. "Can I get you something to eat or drink?" she asks, looking at Pierre and then Tasha, and definitely avoiding eye contact with me.

"We'd love some pastries," Tasha says. "And I'm guessing these two would take espresso with their baked goods. I'll go for whatever herbal tea you think is good. Let me come help you."

Tasha stands and follows Heather toward the espresso

machine and pastry display at the back of the shop. Pierre fixes his attention on me.

"What?" I ask.

"You can't help yourself, can you?" Pierre asks. He's smiling, but he's got the look of a dad who's giving a lecture he's given one too many times.

"Help myself?"

"You have to flirt with every woman you see."

"First of all, you know me better than that. What I just did was not flirting. Secondly, no. I do not have to flirt with every woman I see. That woman, though ..."

"Is my sister-in-law," Pierre says.

"Right. Yes. I hear you."

"She's been through a lot," Pierre's tone is soft and confidential.

I can only imagine she has. She's a single mother, which means she obviously lost her husband, left him, or he left her. That is, if Nate's father was her husband. Maybe Heather got pregnant without ever being married. I'm mentally filling in a lot of blanks that are not my business to fill.

"Her ex cheated," Pierre tells me. "And she's the staple here. She runs this business as if it were her own. The owners have been talking of selling for over a year. When anyone thinks of Catty Coffee, they think of Heather. She's the heart of the shop. And she's a good mom. But she has so much bread on the board. More than one woman should." Pierre pauses to let his talk sink in. "Heather's one of the strongest and kindest women I know."

I nod, feeling a lot like I did when my father used to lecture me about the proper way to treat women when I was a boy. I'll admit I needed the reminder—maybe both then and now. It's not like I would ever treat a woman poorly, but Heather may not need my flirting as much as she needs me to keep my distance. I'll bear that in mind going forward.

"Excuse me," I say to Pierre. Then I scoot my chair out and walk to the back of the shop so I can patiently stand at the counter where Heather and Tasha are making espressos and talking in the comfortable way good sisters do.

"Can I help you?" Heather asks me. Her tone is professional, but warm.

"I am only here to help carry the food to our table."

"Oh. Okay."

She looks a little shocked at my offer. Then she gives me a soft smile before turning to place a croissant on a plate next to two other plates with cheese danish and a muffin. She hands the plates over to me. Our eyes meet and she glances away.

I turn and carry the plates to our table. It makes no sense that I would feel drawn to Heather. Women were asking me to dance throughout the night last weekend. I have female friends who regularly text me to ask me to lunch or drinks multiple times each week. Yet not one of them has stirred this strange feeling I'm having when I look at my best friend's sister-in-law.

I had forgotten how subtly beautiful Heather is. And the way she instantly puts me in my place; I'm not used to it. Most women find me engaging and charming. Discovering one who grabs my attention and holds it in any way beyond friendship has been impossible.

But Heather intrigues me. Even before Pierre told me about her past, I had sensed her inner strength and independence. We met both times I visited before. Once for the initial sham wedding between Pierre and Tasha, and again when they renewed their vows at a second, sincere ceremony.

I set the three dishes of pastry on the table, reserving the croissant for myself and leaving the other two plates for Pierre and Tasha to choose from.

I glance back at Tasha and Heather as I take my seat across from Pierre.

Heather's tucking a strand of hair behind her ear while she's speaking to Tasha. The smile on her face is easy and genuine. She's this juxtaposition of soft and strong that I find oddly alluring. And inconvenient. My best friend is her brother-in-law. We're practically related. Not to mention, we live on different continents. Highly inconvenient.

I take a bite of the croissant. It's not as good as the ones back home, but I'm surprised at the flakiness and lightness of the pastry. I've had the misfortune of eating American croissants that had the consistency of a muddy boot. This one is not disappointing. I wonder if Heather bakes these here, or if she has them brought in.

Tasha returns to our table while Heather mingles with customers and then, finally, Heather takes the seat between me and Pierre.

"I can't sit for long," she says, apologetically.

"Would you like something to eat while you join us?" I offer.

"No. No. I don't eat while I'm working. I'll eat later."

I don't argue, though I have an overwhelming urge to nudge my half-eaten croissant in her direction. Better yet, I could cook for her. I shake my head lightly and sip my espresso, hoping the shot of caffeine will clear my muddled thoughts.

4

HEATHER

Life is a continual process
of having the rug pulled out from under your feet.
~ Pema Chödrön

"Okay, Floyd. I'll see you later."

I give one of my favorite customers a smile and turn to head back toward the counter before the mid-morning rush. Yes. We have a mid-morning rush. Moms come in after dropping their kids to school. Community college students come in to study. Local authors and entrepreneurs come in to work amidst the indistinct buzz of conversation and overhead music.

"Not if I see you first, baby girl," Floyd quips back to me.

My regulars, people. They think it's comedy night every morning. I love that man, though. Too bad he's old enough to be my grandpa. Most good men are. I figure by the time they've reached sixty-five, they've given up trying to impress and what you see is what you get. If only everyone were so easy to read. People should come with nutritional labels, only instead of protein, fat and calories, the labels would say integrity, thoughtfulness, sense of humor. Things like that.

"What's got you smiling?"

I look up and smile even wider at a face I've known almost as long as my own. My best friend, Hannah, is dressed like she's a model for some chic winter catalog. She's wearing knee-high leather boots, with a darling, tailored jean skirt and a tan and black tartan peacoat wrapped over the top of it all.

"You are a vision," I say.

"Could you pass that memo to Huddy?"

"He's blind. And dumb."

"You know he's not dumb. I don't find foolish men attractive."

"Well, any man who hasn't pursued you like the first batch of apple cider donuts in fall is a fool if you ask me."

"He's focused."

"Never, and I repeat, never, make excuses for a man."

"I hear you." Her playful expression falls.

I was the queen of making excuses for Andrew. Until I realized I had been excusing extracurriculars and unconsciously conspiring with him to hide the truth of his indiscretions from myself.

"Don't let me poop in your Cheerios. Huddy will wake up. And, if he doesn't, you will move on. Because I'll make you."

"You will, won't you?"

"That's what girlfriends are for."

"And moms."

"And moms." I smile. "Now. What can I get you?"

Hannah orders her usual, our butterscotch oat milk latte. While I make the espresso for her drink, she lingers at the counter and we chat.

"What grown man still goes by his high school nickname, anyway?"

"Huddy." Her voice sounds way too dreamy for my flavor.

"It's wrong. He should have switched to Hudson once he graduated. That's a perfectly respectable grown man's name. What if his name had been Timothy? Should we still be calling him Timmy? Nothing commands respect in the boardroom like Timmy calling the meeting to order. I picture a five year old named Timmy having to stand on the chair while taking a bite of his PBJ sandwich and then leaving the meeting for his afternoon nap. Huddy sounds like a teen YouTuber."

"Stahhhp."

I've got Hannah laughing at my half-teasing monologue.

But seriously, *Huddy?*

"He's in construction. He doesn't run a boardroom."

"I know what the manchild does," I tease.

Hannah rolls her eyes. "He has a nickname. He's no child."

And again with the dreamy eyes. I'm surrounded by hopeless romantics.

"Ooooh," she says, as I set her coffee in front of her. "I heard Pierre's friend was in town."

"You heard, huh? Yes. Rene is visiting for three weeks. He's staying at Tasha and Pierre's."

"I heard that too. So ..."

"So, what?"

"So, are you spending time with him?"

"He'll probably come to family dinner. He was in here

yesterday, kissing everyone on the cheeks and acting all flirty as Frenchmen do."

"That's such a stereotype. Are you really going there?"

"True. My brother-in-law is the ultimate gentleman. So, not all Frenchmen are shameless flirts. But definitely that one. He's got whatever the French word for danger is written all over him. He's like setting a chocolate cake in front of a diabetic. She'll enjoy the experience and ... then she'll die."

"Oh! My! Gosh!" Hannah is laughing hard now.

I love making her laugh. She's too easy.

When Hannah catches her breath, she asks, "So ... Rene went around kissing everyone? Man, why didn't you call me?"

I nearly blush, and I'm not sure why.

"Not everyone."

"Ohhh?"

Here's the problem with life-long friends. They know you—like, really, really know you. And right now, Hannah's little inquisitive brain can see right through me. She knows darn well I'm the only one Rene kissed.

"Anyway, what are you up to today?" I deflect.

"Oh no. No. Nope. You're not going to wiggle out of this story, missy."

I chuckle. "Can't blame a girl for tryin'."

"True enough. So ... he kissed your cheeks?"

"That's what they do. It's a French thing, and that's not a stereotype."

"I know that. I'm just saying, what was it like? Like, was it all casual, a bit formal, or did he look at you a certain way?"

I may as well get this over with. Hannah's eyes go soft and she takes a sip of her coffee. She knows I'm about to cave. A couple walks up to the counter, "Thanks so much,

Heather." They set their dirty mugs off to the side in the spot I have designated.

"You two have a great day."

As soon as they are out of earshot, Hannah's brows raise and her eyes twinkle in anticipation. I'm prematurely sorry to disappoint her. I'm still me. Even if Rene did look at me a certain way, it wouldn't matter. Because, one: he's a man. Two: he's a flirt. And, three: he's from another country. But I'll humor my bestie. It will basically make her overly-romantic day.

"So, he was sitting with Pierre and my sister. I came over. When I got there, Tasha said, 'You remember Rene.' I said something like 'Who could forget?'"

"You didn't! That's classic. You know those are words that tell him you've taken notice."

"Taken notice that he's an incurable flirt."

"Go on."

"Okay. Anyway, instead of just saying something normal like, 'Good to see you again, Heather,' Rene gets up out of his chair, rounds the table and kisses me on both cheeks."

"But was it like, *Hi. I'm a Frenchman. Good to see you.*? Or was it like, *Hey cutie, I remember you too. Oh boy, do I.*?"

Now it's my turn to laugh. And yes. It was more like option B. I debate trying to pull the wool over my best friend's eyes. It won't work.

"Closer to B. He stared at me like a wolf to a lamb. Then he put his hands on my shoulders, probably to make sure I wouldn't run off. Then he kissed each side of my face lightly."

I can still feel the places where he kissed me when I talk about it, but I'm for sure taking that little embarrassing and uncomfortable truth to my grave.

"Ooooh." Hannah nearly bounces on her toes. She takes another sip of her latte and waits for more tidbits. "Did he say anything?"

"Um. Yeah."

"What did he say?" She's nearly squeaking as she asks.

"He said, 'You look beautiful this morning.'"

"He said *that*?"

"Which he'd say to you, probably had already said to my sister, and would even say to Peggy Grady, too."

Hannah laughs lightly. Peggy Grady is one of our town gossips, and beautiful isn't the first adjective that would come to mind on a first impression.

"Mm mm. I don't think so. I think he noticed that you are beautiful. And he had the guts to say it. I respect that in a man."

"You respect lechery?"

Hannah shakes her head. Then she leans in a little closer.

"I know you were burned. That's a him problem, not a you problem. We've been over this, but I'll say it until my vocal cords rot. Just because a guy convinced us all he was made of better stuff and turned out to be a two-timing ..." She takes a deep breath. I adore that she gets even more riled up over Andrew's cheating than I do. "Well ... that does not mean you should take yourself off the market for good. You deserve more."

"I have more. I have Nate, and you, and Tasha. I've got sweet parents. And I've got this place. That's a whole lot of more. I've got so much more I can barely keep up with all my more. I don't need to add a man to that list to make it complete."

"I hear you. And I agree. Women can be completely

fulfilled single. Look at us. We're happy and we rock life in our early thirties. I just have this feeling you're holding back. And that's the part I want to see you give up. Be open to the possibility. You don't even have to go looking. Just don't lock the gates so tight that a good man can't get through if he comes knocking."

"Okay." I say the word to quell my bestie, not because I'm unlocking gates anytime soon. She probably knows that. But being the good friend she is, she lets it go—for now.

"I better run," Hannah says. "I'm staging a sale for one of the old craftsman homes today."

Hannah's an interior designer, among other things. She also teaches pilates at a little studio a few blocks down from Catty Coffee a couple nights a week. And she paints. A few of her paintings are for sale in local galleries. I've even hung some on the walls to sell for her here at the shop. I had to talk her into starting to sell. She said she just paints for the mental health break, but she's truly talented, and I knew she wanted to step out of her comfort zone and sell. She just needed the nudge.

Hannah and I definitely have a history of nudging one another to take healthy risks. We always have. I just wish she weren't trying to nudge me into being open to dating. Thankfully, no one's lining up to ask me out, so the problem isn't one I'll be facing in the foreseeable future.

The bell over the door jingles right after Hannah walks out, and a group of five walks in. The middle-aged couple look around like they're doing an inspection. When they step further into the shop, I recognize the older couple behind them right away. Stan and Melanie—the owners of Cataloochee. I walk toward them, smoothing my hands down my apron as I go. It's not that Stan and Melanie don't love me. They do. A lot. It's just, they never come into the shop. Ever. They trust me implicitly to run every aspect of the business for them. They have me send them the financials every month. Otherwise, I hire, fire, train, stock, open, close, and run everything.

"Oh, Heather! How good it is to see you!" Melanie says.

Melanie's got a motherly way about her, but she's a mother who eats only grass-fed meat, makes her own granola, and wears Birkenstocks year-round. She still kayaks several times a week even though she's nearing seventy years old, and she's the chairman of the local bird watchers in the Audubon Society.

"Hi, Melanie. What a pleasant surprise to see you. Can I get you all something to eat, or drink? Both?"

"I love what you did there," Stan says, pointing to my window decor honoring the upcoming holiday. Then he looks at Melanie and says, "I've been meaning to ask you if you'd be my valentine."

"Oh, hush up. You know I'll be your valentine. Like I have a choice."

She gives him heat, but you can tell she loves him in the way only a couple who has weathered decades together does.

"Oh, whew," Stan says, looking at me and winking. "I thought she might say no this time."

Melanie rolls her eyes. Then she leads the group to one of the tables along the far wall. "Come talk with us a minute, Heather."

I follow along dutifully, feeling like a pig being led to slaughter. I'm not usually superstitious, but something feels ominous about this whole experience.

"Heather, this is Mark. He's a realtor who specializes in commercial properties. He's from Asheville."

"Hi, Mark," I say. "Can I get everyone drinks?"

Realtor? Commercial realtor? I stare at the sugar packets in their little basket near the wall. If there's a commercial realtor in the building with a younger couple, this whole situation doesn't math well. It's adding up to new ownership. Will they want to keep the coffee shop open? Do they have another business in mind? Will they keep me on, or will I be unemployed?

My head feels light, and my knees, which are strong enough to keep me from swooning over a certain Frenchman, are feeling suddenly ready to buckle.

"Sit down, Heather. We'll have drinks in a bit. Or, why don't you have ..." Stan points to my part-time employee—well, *his* employee technically—Jared.

"Jared?" I supply.

"Yes. Yes. Jared. Why don't you have Jared come take our orders."

Most customers order coffees at the counter, but these are the owners. I signal to Jared. He takes everyone's orders. And I reluctantly take a seat. Stan and Melanie are good people. It's been a dream running this shop for them.

I started working here part-time in high school just to make a little extra money. Then I went to Community College for business. It was a practical degree, and I wanted to eventually have a bachelors to my name. I worked part-time through those two years—including the year before I graduated with my Associates. That's the year I met Andrew. He was passing through town one day after hiking the trails on the outskirts of Harvest Hollow. Andrew grew up in Asheville. He started showing up at Cataloochee regularly on weekends after that first day he ordered coffee from me. After a few weeks, he started lingering around chatting long after he finished his coffee.

When Andrew finally asked me out, I stumbled over my words. I couldn't say yes quickly enough. I never did have any sort of game when it came to men. Andrew chuckled at my awkward reaction like I was the cutest thing he'd ever seen, bungling my words, and blurting out a rapid yes to a date as if I'd never been on one.

After our first date, Andrew came up to see me regularly, sending flowers to the shop during the week, and inviting me to Asheville to hang out with him occasionally. When he landed a job here in town for an outfitter that runs expeditions on the local rivers and trails, we thought it was fate. He was my dream guy. Until he became my nightmare.

I kept working at Cataloochee, or Catty Coffee, as the locals call it, throughout our marriage, through my pregnancy and even after I gave birth. When Nate was two, Stan and Melanie approached me. *We're in our sixties. We need to start backing off the business.* I had already been opening and closing for them a few days a week. Andrew could flex his hours, and we tag-teamed so I could take on more here at the shop while still parenting Nate. I thought we made a great partnership until Andrew went rogue and decided he wanted more—or different, or extra. I never will know what he was looking for that I couldn't be for him. Nate was three when Andrew and I separated. Nate turned four when the divorce was final. I've been running the shop all that time.

Why is my brain going on this strange stroll down memory lane?

"You understand. Don't you, Heather?" Stan asks me.

"I'm sorry. Could you repeat that last part?"

How did I space out at the most critical moment? I have no idea what Stan just said.

"This is a little overwhelming, isn't it?" Melanie says, putting her hand on mine.

"A little," I admit.

"I'll just back up to the beginning," Stan mercifully says. "We've been telling you we're thinking of selling for over a year now. And, well. It's time. We contacted Mark last week. He had reached out a while ago and he's been patiently waiting for our go-ahead. And these two ..." The younger couple at the table smile at me. "... well, they are interested. Possibly. This is Garrett and this is Livvy."

"Hi. Nice to meet you." I put on a smile. After all, these may be my new bosses one day.

"So, we thought we'd come up and show them around and let them see the place in action."

I sit quietly, not sure what to say.

Jared brings everyone's drinks. Garrett and Livvy keep looking around. Their eyes scan the whole building and the customers. They look at me, at Jared, at the coffee station. Eventually, Mark, Stan and Melanie take them on a tour including the kitchen and the back office. Then Garrett, Livvy and Mark leave, and Stan and Melanie linger behind.

"We know this still might feel a bit jarring, Heather. And everything's all just in the talking stages. Nothing's formal."

Melanie's hand is on my arm again, and I know she means to comfort me, but I'm feeling like I'm on the verge of tears.

I nod.

"We sure wish we could just leave it to you and Nate." Melanie's eyes are soft and compassionate.

"No. No. I understand. I'm not family."

"Heather," Stan says. "You're as close to being family as someone can get."

"Thank you."

"We aren't making any decisions. We'll talk to you if things get serious."

Like they aren't serious now? We just said goodbye to a realtor and potential buyers.

"Okay. I appreciate that."

Melanie leans in and gives me a hug.

Stan winks at me. "We sure appreciate you."

"Thanks."

I'd say more, but I need to keep my composure.

Melanie and Stan leave and I stare after them wondering why it seems life is yanking yet one more rug out from under me.

5

RENE

Never doubt the courage of the French.
They were the ones who discovered snails are edible.

~ Doug Larson

"It's so good to see you again, Rene."

Tasha's mom, Louisa, is puttering around the kitchen, but she stops and sets down her wooden spoon when Pierre, Tasha and I walk into the room. I approach her and give her cheek kisses. She brings her hands to her face and her shoulders rise just the slightest. A blush creeps across her neck.

"Oh, my. I don't think I'll ever get used to that greeting."

"Calm down, dear," Tasha's dad, Don, says with a soft chuckle. Then he turns to us. "Can I get you anything to drink? Heather and Nate should be here any minute and I won't be able to get a word in edgewise once my grandson arrives. He's the star of the show around here. So get your requests in to me now."

We tell Don what we'd like and then I offer to help with dinner.

"You need to stop all that kissin' of my wife's cheeks and offering to help. She's going to start upping her expectations, and I don't think I can compete with a young Frenchman." Don jokes while he takes glasses down from the cupboard.

"You've got nothing to worry about, Hun," Louisa says to Don. "I never expected you to be anything more than what you are." They exchange a smile and then Louisa turns to me. "Here, Rene. Take this pan of potatoes in and set it on the sideboard in the dining room."

I take the hot casserole dish, adjusting my grip on the potholders, and bring it into the dining room where hotpads are lined and waiting for the food to arrive. The front door in the living room opens and I turn to see Heather and Nate walking in, bundled in coats and scarves.

Nate takes off his coat and shucks it onto the floor. Heather gives him a warning glance and he bends to pick it up.

"You're here too, Mister Rene!" Nate says as he places his jacket on a rung on the front coat rack.

"I am." I spread my arms wide to reinforce my obvious presence.

Heather's eyes catch mine and I don't look away. Instead, I smile softly at her, remembering Pierre's words about her ex-husband. My admiration for her couldn't be stronger. I don't know if I should greet her with kisses, but habit, and maybe something else, propels me forward. I grip Nate first, bending to place two air kisses on either side of his face.

"Gross!" he shouts. But he's smiling. "We don't kiss in America!"

"You don't?" I chuckle.

Nate doesn't bother expounding on his thoughts. He runs past me toward the kitchen yelling something about what he hopes his grandma made for dessert. The conversation in the kitchen filters out toward the living room, but Heather and I are alone, making my greeting for her feel oddly intimate.

"Good to see you, Heather. Bonne soirée." I lean in and kiss each of her cheeks, forcing myself not to linger. The moment is over quickly, but Heather stands still, staring at me with a slightly dazed look on her face.

"May I take your coat?"

"I've got it," she says quietly.

Her usual fire seems to be burned down to embers. Perhaps she is tired. Or something else is weighing on her.

Aware that I don't want to cause her discomfort or make her feel awkward, I step back. She walks toward the kitchen and I follow her. We appear in the doorway together and everyone's conversation stops, looking from me to Heather and back again.

"I didn't bring anything," Heather says in an apologetic tone.

"No worries, Hun." Louisa flits from the stove to the island and back. "I've got enough to feed all of us and the neighbors should anyone stop by. Are you alright?"

Louisa stops and searches her daughter's face.

"It's just ... been a day. How can I help?"

"You can put your feet up until the meal is ready," Don says with a tone that doesn't leave room for argument.

"Thanks," Heather says.

She and Tasha disappear into the living room. I hear Tasha asking Heather what's going on. Heather tells Tasha something like, *It's too big to go into right now. I don't want to ruin dinner.* Then their voices become indistinct and I can't make out anything else.

Pierre steps over to me and softly asks, "As-tu fait quelque chose qui rend les choses gênantes?"

"No!" I whisper firmly. "Why do you assume I would be the cause of her distress? I didn't do anything to make her feel awkward."

Pierre nods. He has a smirk on his face. Yes. I'm flirtatious at times, but I'm mature enough to know when to hold back. His warning from yesterday lives in my head. I would like nothing more than to befriend Heather and be the type of person she could consider leaning on if she has a hard day. But I'll be leaving in two and a half weeks. I don't have much to offer her, so I will offer my polite distance. She obviously has the best people here who all care for her very well.

"Well now," Louisa says, "Everything's ready."

She directs us four men, including Nate, to each grab a platter or bowl and we carry all the food to the dining room. Heather and Tasha join us. Tasha's arm is around Heather's shoulder in a comforting embrace when they appear at the table. I'm far too curious about the details of Heather's life. It's not like me to be this preoccupied with a woman I barely know.

Dinner conversation focuses around Nate trying out for the town junior softball team, an upcoming Valentine's dance and fundraiser at a local farm, and Pierre's next novel. I'm mostly quiet, stealing glances at Heather at times, watching her as she smiles at her family, or when she gently corrects Nate for interrupting conversation.

Her strength makes me proud, which is odd. She's not mine to feel proud of. And the obvious vulnerability she's trying to hide draws up this unfamiliar desire to care for her. Pierre looks over at me with a question on his face. I smile and scoop some potatoes into my mouth. Nothing to see here. Just a dinner guest eating his root vegetables.

"Oh!" Louisa says, looking at Heather. "I bumped into Brennan at the hardware store the other day. Brennan Stropes."

Heather nods.

"He's still single," Louisa adds with a poignant look in her daughter's direction.

"Worse fates have fallen on a man," Heather mumbles.

I'm beginning to wonder if that's true. These days, being single feels less like a gift and more like a sentence.

"I told him to stop by Cataloochee," Louisa continues.

"He's in there all the time, Mom."

"Well, I told him to stop by for something other than coffee." She wags her eyebrows in a very non-discrete gesture.

Heather doesn't roll her eyes, but her tone reminds me of someone in high school being set up by her parents.

"Mom, you didn't."

"You mean Mister Brennan should get some danish?" Nate jumps into the conversation.

Tasha chuckles and covers her laugh with a cough.

Louisa smiles one of those accomplished smiles worn by every well-intentioned matchmaker. She doesn't say a word.

Heather glances at her son, and then back at her mom.

Then she says, "Yes. Danish. And when Mister Brennan comes in, I'll let you ring him up, okay, Nater Potater?"

"Really?!" Nate's obviously giddy with the opportunity to play storekeeper.

Heather glances at her mom over Nate's head and says, "Absolutely."

Whew. Well played.

Heather glances at me, giving me a warning look even though I'm innocently sitting by, overhearing a conversation I didn't ask for or initiate. I smile calmly at her and she shakes her head lightly before turning her attention back to the few remaining bites on her plate.

* * *

The next day, Pierre is busy writing, and Tasha has gone into Asheville to do some recording work for a book she is narrating. I feel useless and nearly as lonely as I do at night in Avignon, so I borrow Pierre's car and take the short drive into downtown Harvest Hollow.

I know better than to hang around Cataloochee. It would make me seem desperate and clingy. So, I take my satchel with my laptop to a little book shop called Book Smart. I peruse the bookshelves and strike up a conversation with the owner, Emmy. I end up purchasing an autobiography of Andy Griffith, a TV star who was born in North Carolina. At the register I throw in a local guide called "What To Do Around Harvest Hollow and the Surrounding Blue Ridge Communities."

I leave my car parked in front of Book Smart and find myself walking toward Cataloochee, almost as if my feet have a mind of their own. The coffee shop is the place I know best here. Besides, an espresso and a croissant would be nice. I only had coffee and yogurt this morning. In France I don't eat between meals, but I'm feeling drawn to live like an American today. Of course, I'd never become an American as Pierre has done. I'm a Frenchman through and through. But a day dabbling in American habits will be a fun change of pace.

Heather is nowhere to be seen when I walk into Cataloochee. The now-familiar warm smell fills the air, making me feel nostalgic and comfortable. The couch by the window is open, so I drape my coat over the back and leave my computer bag while I walk to the counter and put in my order. A young man wearing a hand-painted name tag that says Cedar rings me up and tells me he'll bring my food over when he's got my espresso ready.

Heather emerges from the back of the shop just after I've taken my seat. Our eyes lock like they're two pieces of a magnetic puzzle, finding their counterpart and snapping into place, almost against their wills.

I smile softly, hoping to send the message that I'm not here specifically to see her. Of course I'm not. I'm here for the croissant and a place to feel less alone while I read about a man from North Carolina. Don't mind me. Just another tourist out for some caffeine.

Heather doesn't smile, but she also doesn't look away. And now we're in an odd sort of staring match—one so obvious, Cedar looks over his shoulder to discern what I'm staring at after he sets my plate of pastry in front of me. When he sees it's his boss capturing my attention, he smiles.

"She's single," he unhelpfully quips.

"Yes. I'm aware. But I'm only here for a few weeks."

"Ah. Well, sometimes a little fun is fun."

I chuckle, my eyes still on Heather, who has now looked down and seems slightly flushed. She's tucking a strand of hair behind her ear and looking around for something to occupy herself. I look at Cedar.

He shakes his head. "Nevermind. Heather's not the fun type." He realizes how this sounds. "I mean, she's great. A great boss. Great mom. She's just not the type to date. Or ... have much fun. Okay. Well. Anything else I can get you?"

"No. Thank you." I smile at Cedar.

My mind retraces his words. Is she really that dull? She seems to be the most interesting person I've met so far here in America. I bet she'd be a lot of fun on a date. And just because she doesn't make a habit of dating doesn't mean she shouldn't go out and have a little diversion from her responsibilities.

I put all those thoughts aside. Not my business.

I pick up my laptop and log into the office to check on a few sales that are pending. Once I see that all the paperwork is in order, I send an email to the primary agent covering my clients. Then I close my computer and take up the book about the TV star.

I sit at the shop for a few hours. The lunch crowd comes and the shop bustles to life. Nearly every table is filled and I entertain myself watching Heather move from customer to customer, back to the counter, and then around the room—everywhere but the couch. She makes brief eye-contact with me occasionally, but she never even approaches me to say hello.

At around two o'clock, the crowd has thinned and only a few tables are still occupied. I'm about to pack up when the bell over the door tinkles and Nate comes barreling through.

He starts toward the back of the shop, but then he spots me and turns toward the couch.

"Mister Rene! Why are you here?"

"I came to find a place to read. And to have a croissant."

"That's my favorite. Way better than the muffins!"

I chuckle. "How was your day?"

"Okay. Except a girl in my class told me to be her valentine. I tell these girls and tell these girls I don't like Valentine's Day. They don't even listen." He's got an adorable pout on his face like being chased by women is a hardship. I try to remember life at his age. I can't really place a time I didn't enjoy a little female attention.

"Mom and I both hate Valentine's Day," Nate adds.

"You do?"

Heather walks over now that her son is here.

"Hey, Nater Potater. How was your day?"

"Okay." He throws himself back against the cushions and lands with a dramatic flop.

"Wow. The details just flow out of you," Heather teases.

"Nate was just explaining how you both hate Valentine's Day."

"You were, were you?" She winks at her son. Then she looks at me. "I don't hate it. I just find it ..."

"Silly?" I ask.

"Yes. I guess."

"My sentiments exactly. I just said that exact thing to your sister and Pierre the other day."

"You didn't! Tasha must have been so riled up. What did she say?"

"She obviously loves the holiday. And she had Pierre declaring his admiration for the day too. It was entertaining to watch him."

"I bet. My sister is a hopeless romantic."

"Hopeless? Is romance so hopeless?"

Nate nearly yawns. He stretches to remind us of his presence, and then he says, "Mom, can I please eat a croissant with my homework?"

"It's *may*. *May* I please eat a croissant."

Nate rolls his eyes.

"And, yes. You may. But wash your hands before you eat and use the tongs to take it out of the case."

"Kay." Nate dashes off the couch, leaving me and Heather to finally talk.

"What was I saying?" Heather asks.

"You were saying that romance is hopeless."

"It's fine. Romance, I mean. It's just not all it's cracked up to be. Most people feel initial fireworks, but then that dies off and they are left with a whole lot of reality. Nothing glamorous in that."

"Mmmm," I hum, thoughtfully. "But do you know people who have had the fireworks, as you call it, for more than their beginning season of love?"

"Sure. My sister and your best friend seem to be doing fine."

"Fine? They are so in love. It's not merely fine. They have found true love. Out of all the people on earth, they have found the one they can confide in, the one they can dote on, the one they call their own. And, from what I see, they bring out the best in one another. Pierre is more content now. He was never what I would call restless, but he was ... lacking something. And now, I see. It was Tasha. She is the one he was missing all along."

"You believe in that? In one person. A soulmate?"

"Mmm. Not a soulmate, maybe. But definitely there are people we are destined to meet. Or maybe they are just the right fit. And when we meet that one, we know. And then we should do whatever it takes to pursue them and never let them forget what they mean to us. Because that kind of love is not always so common."

"That's a romantic notion."

"Oui. But it is not wrong."

I look into her brown eyes. I see a woman at war, and not with me. Maybe she wants to believe in romance but this man she had married has completely ruined it for her. *Comme c'est tragique.* Yes. Very tragic. A beautiful young woman should believe in romance. Not only believe, she should experience it.

"Maybe I am more prone to romantic ideas because I am French?"

"Are you saying the French are more romantic than Americans?"

Her tone is lively and challenging, as if the embers that were dying down last night have sparked into a flame again. I love seeing this fire in her. She seems to enjoy coming back to life as much as I enjoy being a witness. There is little I relish more than a friendly verbal sparring match with someone I respect and like.

"Oui. I think we are."

I don't know if we are, but I won't say that now. To concede would be to end this time with her.

"You don't even really celebrate Valentine's Day in France, do you?"

"We do. It's just something between the adults. Our children are not forced to craft cards and tote them to school. Nate would love the fact that he gets a free exemption from the holiday in my country. As for the adults, we will buy chocolat or go away for a weekend. We do not make a show of the day the way you do. But we French men make a point to celebrate the women we love, and each man showers his beloved with affection and attention. Then again, we are raised to do that without a special holiday."

Heather's expression is neutral, but a pink hue tints her cheeks and neck. She likes the idea of being doted on as much as she is fighting it. So, I push gently.

"We don't need Valentine's Day in France. We invented romance."

I pause, not seeing Nate's nearness until it's too late.

Still under the impression that Heather is my only audience, I playfully ask, "Why do you think they call it French kissing?"

Nate surprises me and Heather, drawing our gazes off one another and onto him. "What is French kissing? Do we have American kissing? Ewww. Is French that kissing you tried to give me at Gramma's house? That's gross."

I smile and nod. "Yeah. Totally gross."

I look at Heather and wink. Very slowly, while holding her gaze, I say, "Very gross, right Cher?"

Then I pick up my book and resume reading while she gathers my dirty dishes and walks back to the counter at the rear of the shop.

I watch her go, wishing I were clever enough to have found a way to make her stay a little longer, but knowing I have no business thinking thoughts like that where Heather is concerned.

6

HEATHER

Sadly, no matter how many people you meet,
it's the ones who let you down
who get the best parts of you.
~ R. M. Drake

Cedar is standing outside Cataloochee when I arrive to open for the day.

What's he doing here?

His girlfriend, Jessa, should be here for her shift in an hour, and Cedar isn't scheduled to start work for three hours.

"Hey, Cedar." I stick my key in the lock and open the door, shaking the chill off as I step into the dark shop. I hit the lights on the wall nearest us and a warm glow fills the front of the room.

"Hey, boss, uh ... Heather."

I glance over at Cedar. He's got his hands stuffed into his pants pockets. His shoulders are drawn up a little.

"Are you okay? You know Jessa's working early today. You don't have to be here til seven."

"I know ... and ... uh ... that's the thing."

"What's the thing? Is everything okay? Is Jessa alright?"

I'm talking, but I'm also moving through the shop, turning on lights, adjusting the thermostat, hitting power switches on machines. I pause to look at Cedar again.

"Well. Yes. But no. Well, actually, definitely yes." Cedar's standing a few feet away from me looking like he just robbed a bank.

I can't help propping both hands on my hips. It's four am. It's cold. I have a list a mile long to complete before customers start pouring in, and then I have to leave to wake my son from his cozy, snug bed to get him off to school before I come back here to help with the morning rush.

"Uh. Well. You see, Jessa and I ... well, we've always loved the Appalachian Trail."

"Mm hmm."

This fact is not new to me. It's also totally not newsworthy. Most people in this area love the trail. We live a little over an hour from points where it passes through North Carolina. We're a community of nature lovers.

"We've always wanted to hike the trail."

"You can. It's right there."

Annnnd ... why are we talking about the trail here and now, before I've even had my first cup of coffee?

Later, I'll kick myself for being so dense. Who shows up at dark-o-thirty in the morning to announce their love for a world-renowned hiking trail? I should see the writing on the wall.

"Right. It is. Right there." Cedar smiles a weak smile. "And that's why we're quitting."

"You're ..." I stand stock still, holding a bag of coffee beans in one hand, my jaw dropped open like I'm tilted back in the dentist chair expanding my lips as far as they can go so he'll get a good view of my molars. I feel myself blink slowly as I shut my mouth.

Cedar's voice comes out quietly, as if reducing his volume will soften the reality.

"We're quitting. We need to train and prep. We're not just going on a day hike. We want to travel a good stretch of the trail. If we end up married and having children, it will be a while before we could do something like this ... Maybe we never would. We want to grab the opportunity while we're young. I have money from when my grandpa passed away. We can live off that ..."

He looks at me with these pleading eyes that almost make me want to assure him it's fine. And it would be fine. Well, fine-ish. No. Nevermind. Not fine. Not remotely fine. Actually it's the farthest thing from fine. How am I going to replace two employees?

And, if I'm honest, the sudden overwhelming urge to curl up and cry isn't only about the stress of having to find two new employees. To be completely transparent, a pang of jealousy is seeping through me like a stain. Cedar and Jessa get to just up and quit a job so they can go galavant down a trail together and roll around in the woods like two young hippies while I have to stay here and do all the hashtag adulting.

It's clear to me now. Cedar's not even giving me notice. He's here at this ungodly hour to quit on the spot.

"Are you quitting now? As in, today? Or is this your two weeks' notice?"

A girl can dream.

"Yeah. Well, I know you've got to get Nate to school. We didn't want to bail on you, so I told Jessa to stay in bed, and I came in to give you our notice. I'll stay until you're back from getting the mini-man off to school. But, after that, we're done. We've read up on hiking the trail. There's a lot to do. We need the freedom to focus on our journey."

"To focus on your journey," I numbly echo.

I can't help myself. I feel tears start to prick behind my eyelids. I'm a grown woman. A manager. A single mom. I weather storms. I lived through infidelity and a divorce. I managed bedtime tantrums and Nate's bouts of the stomach flu with no one by my side. I never lose my marbles or my cool, and now I feel like I'm about to lose them both. The accumulated stress of six years threatens to burst out my tear ducts in some sort of suppressed geyser eruption to rival Yellowstone.

"Excuse me for just a minute ... uh ... please," I mutter before turning so Cedar can't see my face, and walking through the swinging door that leads to the kitchen and office space.

Cedar's voice drifts in behind me. "Take your time. I know I dropped a bomb. I'll get everything set up out here."

I almost say thank you. But I don't. He's such a contradiction—thoughtful, but ultimately leaving me hanging. Kind of like my ex: charming, but unable to keep his vows. If only a person would settle on one end of the spectrum or the other. Why mingle care with rejection? It only muddies the waters. It's the mottled nature of people that makes reading them so challenging and depending on them nearly impossible.

Do small kindnesses really matter when you're being dumped? I'm going with a no on that one. Maybe come back and ask me tomorrow and I might have a different answer.

I fight the inner voice giving me a spontaneous lecture on trust.

You can't trust men.

You can't trust anyone.

Eventually, all people will let you down.

My inner voice should never be asked to give a TED talk, as you can plainly see. I know those thoughts are just reactions to the shock of Cedar and Jessa quitting. I'm old enough and wise enough to discern that I'm not in my right mind right now. I probably shouldn't operate heavy machinery for the next little bit here.

The thing is, I've been left high and dry before. And, I was already feeling vulnerable this week. The future of the shop is completely uncertain, which means I have no way of predicting my life going forward.

And now I'm down two key full-time positions.

It's times like this I wish I had a life partner—someone who could shoulder half the load, who would listen to me rant about employees who quit without notice, who would hold me while I fell apart, and then stick around while I put myself back together.

What's the old saying? *If wishes were fishes we'd have some fried; And if wishes were horses, beggars might ride.* Wishing for someone to walk through life with me won't solve my problems. I'm here, and I'm all I've got.

I flop into my desk chair, noticing a drawing on my desk Nate must have done yesterday. It's me and him and a dog.

We obviously don't have a dog. Nor are we getting one. Could you imagine? Talk about a straw breaking the camel's back. This camel has all the straw she can handle.

I close my eyes, too weary to actually cry. Then I take a few deep breaths and shoot a text off to Tasha. I do have her, even if she's immersed in her life with Pierre and will only be less available when the baby comes. But Tasha is always here for me. I'm not truly as alone as I often feel.

Heather: *Well, you'll never guess what happened.*

Tasha is probably dead asleep, still curled up in Pierre's arms. That thought makes me smile while it also sends an ache straight through me. I used to wake up like that—wrapped in the arms of a man who I thought loved me. Nope. No. Not going there.

I send a second text to Tasha. Then I copy that text and paste it to Hannah.

Heather: *Since you are probably still sleeping, I'll tell you how I started my day. Cedar came in and tendered both his and Jessa's resignations. He's staying here this morning so I can get Nater off to school. But then he's out. They both are. Looks like I'm hiring two baristas. If you know anyone ...*

7

RENE

Sometimes when you meet someone, there's a click.
I don't believe in love at first sight,
but I believe in that click.

~ Ann Aguirre

I t takes me a few moments after I wake to remember I'm in Pierre and Tasha's home in North Carolina. I roll over and stretch. Once I'm dressed, I make my way to the kitchen. Tasha's leaning against one of the counters sipping a cup of coffee. She looks perplexed.

"My recording gig will keep me a little busier than we anticipated over the next few days. I'm sorry," she tells me.

Her job narrating audiobooks is the perfect fit for the wife of a world-renowned author.

"I knew you and Pierre would be busy while I visited. Don't worry about me. I'll find things to do."

"A few friends of mine mentioned wanting to meet you

while you're here." Tasha wags her eyebrows playfully, but then her face looks preoccupied again—maybe because she's got work on her mind.

"I take it you are talking about female friends?" I walk over to the coffee pot and pour myself a cup.

"Yes. All females. As a matter of fact, my friend, Britt, is a real estate agent here in town. She could show you around properties if that's your idea of fun. I bet it would be interesting to see the market in Harvest Hollow as compared to Avignon. None of my friends would consider it a hardship to spend a little time with a charming Frenchman."

I chuckle. "A charming Frenchman. Is that so?"

Tasha smiles. We both know I'm charming.

Normally, I might take her up on an offer like this, but I'm feeling drawn toward the local coffee shop. No one would accuse me of being a creature of habit, and I'm definitely not one to hang around where I'm not thoroughly wanted. Heather hasn't exactly laid out a welcome mat in my honor. Maybe that's what's making me want to go back. I have the typical male urge to conquer a challenge. But as soon as I think that thought, it doesn't sit quite right with me. Something else is pulling me back to Cataloochee.

I'm a man in my early thirties. I've been around women all my life. At this point, I know what I want and what I don't. Up until a few weeks ago, I believed I was satisfied having fun, socializing, and living a life I directed.

No one bothers me.

No one fights with me.

No one lays claim on my time.

Maybe I've been restless longer than I knew. Now that I'm aware, I can't shut down the idea that I'd like more. Obviously, it won't be with an American woman. Still, Heather intrigues me. And I know for certain she lacks fun in her life. She's probably forgotten she's an irresistible woman, and not merely because of her looks. Lucky for her, I am just the man to show her a good time and help her remember she's more than a mom and a female business owner. Heather's a woman. And she deserves to remember that fact.

I take a sip of coffee and consider Tasha's offer. Maybe I should take her up on it just to shake the unexpected pull I'm feeling to watch her sister flit around the coffee shop. How dull is my life that I need to travel to America to watch a barista run her business? This could be a new low.

Tasha pushes off the counter. "I'm going to shower. If you decide to take me up on setting you up with any of my friends, let me know."

I nod and tell her I will. Then I pick up my mug and walk over to the back windows looking out over the deck into the woods. Pierre comes into the living room, looking so at home it nearly shocks me. Of course, he is at home. This is his home now. It would be easier to adjust to the fact if I had seen him fall firsthand. If I'd been around watching him and Tasha build a life here, his ease and familiarity wouldn't be so startling. But I've only visited sporadically. All I know are the empty places Pierre used to fill in Avignon, not the new places he's claimed for himself here.

He lights a fire and settles into one of the overstuffed chairs in their comfortable living room.

"Your wife mentioned some friends of hers wanting to show me around town."

Pierre chuckles. "Ah, yes. She may have some thoughts about how to keep you entertained while you are here."

"I don't need Tasha going out of her way."

"You know how she is when she gets an idea in her head. She's very excited about this little project of hers."

"Project?"

"Oui. Getting you to enjoy yourself with someone while you are here. She even said, 'Who knows, maybe Rene will fall in love while he's in Harvest Hollow.'"

"Oh, I see. Well then, no pressure on me." I chuckle. "Do these friends know they are on the unofficial French edition of *The Bachelor* now?"

"I'm not sure what she told them. That you are French, I'm sure. I've made a great impression. They all think Frenchmen are tres marvellioux. Don't ruin it for me."

"As if I would ruin it for you. Wasn't it always the other way? You were the one I had to warn not to be so dour and reserved when we went out. Women love me."

Pierre laughs. "Women find you entertaining. It's true."

"In all seriousness, I'm only here for three weeks. I'm not seeking romance. I only need the change of pace. You know me better than I know myself, apparently. Being here is good. It is giving me ... perspective. And a much needed rest." I pause, giving my next sentence room to sink in when I say it. "Besides, I am already in love."

Pierre's eyes snap up to mine. "Oh really?"

"Oui. I've found the love of my life." I pause again, watching his reaction with amusement. When enough time has passed, I announce, "I'm in love with France."

"Ahhh. You. Well, I'm glad you at least have an object for all your affection."

I do love France—even if I'm not as fully in love with my life as I used to be. Maybe it's a phase. A little time in America should give me enough homesickness that I long for Avignon and appreciate her all the more when I return.

"What is your day like?" I ask Pierre.

"I'm plotting a novel. And it's my turn to cook dinner, so I'll go to the market. And I should see if I can help out at the coffee shop. What would you like to do?"

"The coffee shop? Do you help out there often?"

This is something I hadn't heard before. I imagined Pierre spending most of his days in his home, writing. And then maybe he would spend the rest of his time promoting books, doing signings and other author things. I didn't know he helped at the coffee shop.

"Oui. Heather is in a bit of a tough spot. Two employees quit this morning without notice. She will have to manage everything until she finds replacements. Tasha almost canceled her recording schedule so she could help her sister until I assured her Heather would have enough support. Heather has two other part-time workers, but these two that quit were her full-time help. I might end up being more in the way than helpful, but I can at least take orders and clear dishes."

"The great Pierre Toussaint is now a busboy." I chuckle.

"For my family, I would do whatever is needed."

Family. The word settles like a lump.

"I could help her aussi."

"Oh, no. You do not have to. You're here on holiday. Relax. We've got Heather covered."

"I thought you just said Tasha was going to be recording."

"She is. But Heather's parents are also going to help out. Between all of us, she'll be fine."

I nod, even though I don't agree. Heather's load is already heavy. Now she has to carry the work of three employees and try to make space in that schedule to interview and hire new help. I'm free. I don't tell Pierre, but I know what I'm going to do.

Less than an hour later, I've borrowed Pierre's car and driven into town. I find a parking spot in front of the General Store next door to Cataloochee Coffee. Nervousness overcomes me as if I'm going on a first date with someone who matters—someone I want to impress.

Maybe I do want to impress Heather. She is my best friend's sister-in-law, after all. But I know myself better than that. Heather's connection to Pierre has nothing to do with these almost delightful nerves buzzing to life as I stroll closer to the coffee shop.

A man passes me and says, "Good morning." His smile is broad and welcoming. I smile back, grateful for a steadying moment before I walk into Cataloochee.

The bell over the entry already feels familiar with its soft tinkling chime. I inhale the warm aroma and shake off my coat. Two younger women are sitting on my couch. One of them—the one facing me—smiles sweetly as I catch her eye. I smile back. My eyes rove the room and land on Heather. She's only two tables away from me, pouring a refill into an older gentleman's mug and laughing at something he says. At least she's laughing. I had pictured walking into a scene where she scurried from table to table, her hair sticking in ten directions, her eyes wild. Of course she's composed. She's unflappable. I've seen this each time I've visited Harvest Hollow. Heather's steady and self-possessed even when life unravels around her.

I take advantage of the fact that she doesn't sense my presence yet. Her jeans hug her hips. Her plain white tennis shoes shouldn't grab my attention, but even they seem to catch my eye and make me want to study her like a masterpiece at the Louvre. She's wearing a brown t-shirt with the coffee shop logo on it. Her light brown hair falls softly around her face, the sunlight through the window accentuates a few of the blonder strands. Her face simultaneously hides and tells so much.

She's attentive, even though she somehow missed my entry. Why is a woman so warm and attentive to everyone, so immune to my presence? When she cares, she gives her whole heart. Her son is still oblivious to her sacrifices for him. But I see what she's given up for his sake. She would do anything for Nate. And Heather's devotion to her customers is unparalleled.

She's beautiful in a way only a woman who has no idea of her appeal can be. Women who pour time and effort into their appearance have a certain allure. It's a practiced image, one built to draw the eye. But a woman who throws herself into motherhood and serving others has a different level of desirability. Heather's looks are naturally captivating. Her heart only magnifies her raw beauty.

And, why am I standing here staring at her?

I clear my throat and start to make my way further into the shop. The movement grabs Heather's attention. Instead of avoiding me as she has been doing, she turns toward me and greets me directly.

"Rene, good to see you again."

"De même, Cher. It's good to see you too."

"Oh, that Cher stuff. Pierre won my sister over with that word alone, I think. But she's a romantic. Things like a Frenchman wielding his pet names make her weak in the knees."

I can't help myself. "And what would make you weak in the knees, Heather?"

I walk toward her, fully intending to kiss both her cheeks in a traditional greeting that would mean more to me than what it usually does. I'm a schoolboy crossing lines the teacher will scold him for later.

"Ah. Ah." Heather holds her hand up toward me like a traffic cop. "None of that kissing on the cheeks. You can just say hello."

"As you wish." I smile at her and wink.

She shakes her head, but the soft smile on her lips betrays the rest of her body language. It is my reward. I want to bring one hundred more like it to her face in the next few hours.

"Well?" I ask. Not dropping my earlier question.

"What would make me weak in the knees?" Heather looks as mischievous as I feel. "Probably the flu."

She smiles at me and then asks, "What can I get you? Or are you just in here to say hello?"

"I would love an espresso and one of your croissants." I don't get to say my next sentence before Heather answers me.

"One cwah-sahhhnt and an espresso coming right up."

She mocks my accent, and surprisingly, I love it. No one mocks me—besides my siblings and Pierre.

I eye the couch again. "I'm not here to relax today. Hold my order. I'll have it later."

"You're not here to relax?"

"No. Pierre told me of your situation. I'm here to help."

Heather sizes me up, pursing her lips and squinting just the slightest. "You definitely aren't going to help me. Find a seat and I'll get you your espresso."

I reach out before I think better of it and grasp her elbow in my hand.

"I want to help. I'll be bored watching you. Let me help you, won't you, Cher?"

"Do you even know how to make coffee?"

I chuckle. I am French. I know how to make coffee. "Oui. I know."

Heather looks put out that I would want to help her, but I can tell she is also relieved. "Okay. You can help."

"Good. Show me what to do. Put me to work."

Over the next hour, Heather instructs me on the basics of making coffee in an industrial-sized machine. I'm forbidden from touching the espresso press. I tease Heather about her strict rules, but follow her request. I pass out pastries, take payments at the register, and finally roll up my sleeves and wash dishes in the oversized kitchen sink.

The door swings open while I'm humming a song to myself and rinsing soap out of a cup. Heather comes through looking worn, but happy.

"Thank you, again."

"You thanked me too many times already. It was no problem. I had fun. Otherwise, my morning would have been spent watching you and reading about Andy Griffith."

"Why would you be watching me?"

She immediately blushes. I love the effect I seem to have on her. It brings me more joy than it should.

"Why wouldn't I be watching you?" I wink.

The part of her that rises to a challenge comes out to play. "Why would you? I'm a small-town, single mom working in a coffee shop. Nothing special."

"Oh, that's where you are totally wrong."

I'm quickly developing a mission for my remaining days in Harvest Hollow. It's not reasonable for the two of us to develop anything but a friendship. Our lives will be intertwined for years to come since my best friend fell for her sister, but we will be like extended relatives, nothing more. What I can do is help Heather to see herself the way I see her—the way most men see her. And I can help her lighten up and release some of the stress she seems to always tote around with her like an invisible weight.

"We're both adults here, Heather, so I will speak plainly. You are an intelligent woman. You hold this shop together, never letting a cup go empty and never allowing any customer to feel neglected. You manage to mother your son with the right balance of care and firmness even though you are surely exhausted at the end of every day. And yet, when I see you—when most men see you—we don't see a harried business owner or a single mom barely hanging on to all the details of her overwhelming life. We see a woman who is captivating, intriguing, and beautiful. And that is why I would be watching you."

"Oh." She turns and moves a few items on the counter. "Well."

Heather looks anywhere but in my eyes. It's fine, I know she heard me. What I said doesn't match the opinion she obviously has of herself. And maybe she's not used to men saying such bold truths to her. They should. She ought to become very accustomed to genuine flattery. I'm going to make sure she sees herself with new eyes during the short time we have together.

But I don't want to make her uncomfortable, so I say, "Now. Show me where these cups go and I will put them away before I meet Pierre to go shopping."

"Okay. Yes. Putting away cups. That's good. Right." Heather still doesn't look at me.

She opens a cupboard and points to the empty space. Then she asks, "Shopping? What are you two shopping for?"

"Pierre and I are cooking dinner." Before I have time to think, I add. "You should join us. You and Nate."

"For dinner?"

"Oui. Why not?"

"Well, Nate has dinner at my folks' house tonight. It's their thing. Once a week, my dad meets him after school and they walk to my parents' home together. The three of them have dinner without me. They think they are giving me a break. I don't really need one, though. Not from Nate, at least."

"So you would be eating alone tonight?"

"Basically, yeah."

"Do you have something amazing planned for this night alone of yours?"

"If by amazing you mean putting on my fluffy, ugly socks and heating a bowl of canned soup, then, yes. Absolutely. Amazing."

"No." I shake my head. "No. No. This won't do. You need to come to your sister's and allow me and Pierre to cook for you. Then you can go put on these ugly socks after we have filled you with good food you did not have to cook for yourself."

Heather is shy for a moment. It's a look that suits her, even though I know she has fire beneath that cool exterior. And then she surprises me. "If you insist."

"I do."

"Okay then. What can I bring?"

"Nothing. Bring yourself. It will be casual. Just the four of us." I like the way that sounds too much.

Heather leaves the kitchen while I finish cleaning up. I put the cups up in the cabinet and stack the saucers next to them. I'm placing the last of the spoons into a slotted drawer when Heather returns to the kitchen carrying a plate with a pastry on it and a smaller cup of what I am sure is espresso. She hands me my coffee and looks me in the eyes as I take the croissant.

Her mouth tips up in a half-smile. "You're dangerous. You know that?"

"Moi?"

"Yes, you. I bet no one says no to you—ever."

"Plenty of people say no to me. I'm in real estate, after all. In sales you take at least ten nos for every yes. And, that's on a good day. Besides, I'm the younger sibling to a sister and a brother. Both of them tell me 'no' enough to last me a lifetime."

"That's not what I mean. I'm talking about women. You get what you want."

She doesn't ask me. It's a statement of fact. And I can't deny that women usually say yes to me. There's no challenge in winning a woman over the moment you meet her. And as much as I enjoy the obstacles being set forth by the woman in front of me, I'd equally like to see her set all that aside to let me in just an inch.

"See. Your not-an-answer is plenty of an answer." Heather crosses her arms over her chest.

"So, I'm now a criminal because women find me attractive and I know how to treat them well?"

She blushes, again. It's a beautiful sight. Better than a sunrise over the Rhone river, or a walk in a field of lavender, or the smell of this fresh espresso and warm croissant. This blush. It's enough to fuel my day.

"Not a criminal. Just dangerous." She clears her throat and walks away.

I stand here wondering what I can do to get her to return —and stay—which is ridiculous because I'm only here for three weeks and she's a woman who deserves a man who can truly be there for her. And she is off limits—limits set by my best friend, who seems mild-mannered until you cross an important line.

From what Pierre says, Heather hasn't had anyone to rely on besides herself. Of course, she has him and Tasha, and her parents. But she doesn't have a person of her own who is simply there for her—someone to put her first, to treasure her, to share life with her in the way a devoted boyfriend or husband would. I can't be that man, but I can help her know one exists, and I can encourage her to see that she's worth giving herself another chance at romance.

8

HEATHER

Being an adult is mostly being exhausted,
wishing you hadn't made plans,
and wondering how you hurt your back.

~ Unknown

"He actually said, '... captivating, intriguing, and beautiful'?"

Hannah sets down the rag she was using to wipe tables and makes a big show of fanning herself. "Frenchmen. I'm telling you."

"Now who's resorting to stereotypes?" I don't roll my eyes, but I feel the strong urge to do whatever the grown woman equivalent of an eyeroll is.

"Right. Right. Still. That man. He's as hot as Matt Rife ... or Henry Cavill ... it's not even fair how cut his jawline is. And how is his hair so perfect? It's really too much."

Hannah saw Rene leaving the shop with Pierre when she showed up for her turn at helping me try to manage without my two full-time employees today. Of course Rene introduced himself. I expected him to fawn all over Hannah, but he surprised me by being cordial and charming, yet a little aloof. Why I care is something I don't have time or energy to get into. Let him dote all over my adorable bestie. She deserves it, and she's the type of woman all men should find irresistible. She's pulled-together and she puts effort into herself, unlike me. I'd like to put effort into myself again sometime. Maybe when I feel more settled and Nate's more self-sufficient.

Hannah's not done with her rave review of Rene. "He's scrumptious. And then he says things like *that?*"

"And he lives in France." I look her in the eyes. "France, Hannah."

"Right. But he's here now. No one's proposing marriage. He just asked you to come eat the dinner he's cooking. Oh, for the love of all things. He cooks! Girl, you need to get ready. You are going to eat with him or ..."

"Stop. Don't go there."

Hannah's notorious for making up ridiculous threats. She'll say something horrid or embarrassing and I'll have no choice but to give in to her demands or face a fate worse than death.

... or I'll run outside and shout, "Free Coffee!"

... or I'll call the fire station and tell them you've got a crush on one of the firemen and I won't mention a name.

... or I'll bring Jaspar's pet goat in here next time I stop by— and let him off leash.

... or I'll buy Nate a kitten.

That last one actually sends a chill of fear up my spine.

Not one of Hannah's threats is ever idle. If she says she's going to do something, she does it. She should have been a politician with her gift of persuasion by means of outlandish manipulation tactics.

"Okay. I won't threaten you ... yet. But you are going. And you're getting ready. Look." Hannah waves her hand around toward all the empty tables. "Those two are leaving, and Floyd's the only one left in here. Let's give him the boot and then I'll help you get ready for this date."

"It's not a date. And I'm ready."

I glance down at myself. My half apron has some splotches from this morning, but I'm taking that off and throwing it in the wash when I get home. I'm wearing a T-shirt, jeans and tennis shoes. My hair probably needs to be brushed after the day I've had. Otherwise, I'm good.

"Oh, no. You're not going like that."

"Like what?"

"Like you don't care. Like you just busted your booty to cover three people's jobs. Like you're not even remotely interested."

All three of those things are basically true. Well, I do care. I just can't afford to.

"We're going to remind you that a red-blooded female lives under that apron and those neutral clothes. You are going to get a little spruced up."

"I don't want to send the wrong message."

"And that message would be?"

"That I'm romantically interested in Rene."

"Define romantically interested."

"Hannah."

"Okay. But tell me you wouldn't want him to kiss both your cheeks again and then possibly let his lips drift a little more to the center of your face, to ... oh, I don't know ... your lips?"

"You are incorrigible. I don't want to kiss Rene. That would complicate everything."

"Let go of your overthinking for just a minute. Close your eyes."

"I'm not closing my eyes. I'm going to see if Floyd needs a refill."

"You aren't. I'm going to tell Floyd he needs to head to Book Smart if he still wants to linger at a coffee shop. He'll understand."

"Don't you dare tell Floyd I have a date."

"Wouldn't dream of it." Hannah winks, but it's the wink of Maleficent or Cruella de Vil.

If Hannah thought blabbing to Floyd would get me to go out with Rene, or do whatever it is she imagines I'll do with him, she wouldn't hesitate for a nanosecond to tell Floyd I'm nearly engaged to the Frenchman. Then she'd explain to me how she did it all for my own good and how she would never do anything to harm me. That much is true. At least she doesn't intentionally harm me. Never. She's got my back. Usually. This afternoon, I'm not so sure.

I try to inconspicuously follow Hannah, grabbing the rag she just set down and re-wiping clean tables so I can eavesdrop on whatever she's saying to Floyd.

She leans in close and nearly whispers in his ear. He chuckles and looks over at me.

"That's just mean," I mumble.

"Oh, no. Don't you fret a bit, Heather," Floyd rambles. "I

understand. You need to clear the room. You've got plans. I wouldn't want to be the reason you missed out on something special."

I give Hannah a mild death glare. It's not an actual death glare. More of a flu glare or a stomach bug glare. I don't want her to die, but a little suffering would be just fine.

Floyd's dutifully standing and walking toward the door. "Oh! I already called my nephew. He might be able to come help you out in place of those two flaky employees who up and quit on ya. I never did trust that guy. A man named after a tree isn't to be trusted. Anyhoo, my nephew's got a job at the library, so it would only be Sundays and Mondays that he'd pitch in."

"Thanks, Floyd. You're the best."

I don't need someone working their off days two days a week. I need someone who knows how to run an espresso machine and a frother and how to decorate the top of a latte with a design that says we went the extra mile to serve our customers. I need someone reliable. That could be my life-motto, come to think of it. Woman: in search of someone reliable. What a low bar I've come to set for myself. But, then again, who knew reliability would be such a rare commodity?

"I am pretty great," Floyd says with a warm smile. "You said it, not me. But I've got to agree. Now, go and get ready for whatever plans you have. Be young while you can. Life keeps rolling by and one day you won't be able to bend to tie your shoe without letting out some sort of noise or another. Now's the time to grab up the fun."

I chuckle at Floyd's odd version of a motivational talk.

Hannah crosses her arms over her chest while a look of

deep satisfaction settles over her face. She would have paid Floyd to say those words, and she didn't even have to.

"Okay, Floyd," I say. "I'll go be young if you'll go be awesome."

"Now that's a deal." He smiles at me.

Hannah and I watch Floyd leave and she scurries over to the door as soon as he's out, twisting the lock and flipping the sign in the window to say, CLOSED.

Then she turns and rubs her hands together in eager anticipation. I have the urge to make a run for it, but I know I can't. In for a penny, in for a pound.

"So, what's next?" she asks. "We need to clean this place and head to my house so I can dress you and do your makeup."

"Hannah. I'm serious. Rene's going to take one look at me and know I changed my clothes and freshened up to impress him—which is not what I'm doing."

"Then tell him I insisted on pampering you. The result will be the same. You'll feel human and desirable. And he'll be unable to keep his eyes off you."

"Which is a good idea because ...?"

"Because he's a hot Frenchman and you are a single mom who hasn't gone on a date in over five years. You need to dust things off, girlfriend. Get out there and have some fun. Lighten up and enjoy the attention of a gorgeous man for a change. It's a no risk investment. You two have an expiration date."

I walk into the kitchen and Hannah follows me. I move from spot to spot, shutting things down, putting things away, opening cabinets and taking quick inventory for tomorrow. She grabs the mop and cleans the front room. For free. I have the best friends and family in the world.

Hannah comes back into the kitchen as I'm finishing my clean up.

I throw my dirty apron in the laundry bin at the back corner of the kitchen. I'll deal with that later this week.

Then I turn to Hannah. "I can't flirt with Rene. First of all, I think my flirter is broken from lack of use. Second of all, he's not just some guy. He's my brother-in-law's best friend. We'll see one another regularly for the rest of our lives."

"But you like him."

Her expression is so hopeful. I love her for it.

"I think he's fun. And ... there's more to him than I saw when we first met. I originally thought he was a womanizing flirt. And then I got to know him a little better the few times he visited and realized I had misjudged him. And then today he came and helped at the shop. Now, he wants to cook me dinner. There's something in the way he always says exactly what he's thinking that makes me think he's sincere."

"And he's gorgeous and he thinks you're captivating."

Those words of Rene's were extravagant. No man has said things like that to me in a long, long time—okay, ever. And I can't afford to listen to flattery. It's like strolling down the boutiques in Chapel Hill to pick out a dress—a dress that would cost the equivalent of my month's wages. I need to be practical and not lose myself in the beautiful words of a man who is here on a three-week vacation. Rene will leave and my life will carry on here—with Nate, and hopefully some form of a job in this shop.

"Obviously, he likes my croissants." I deflect.

"Oh, I bet he likes your croissants."

"Stop it." I'm smiling, but shaking my head.

Hannah giggles at her own joke. "Okay. But humor me.

Let loose a little. Enjoy being the object of someone's compliments and winks for a change of pace."

"I'll consider it."

"That's all I can ask."

Hannah drags me out of Cataloochee after we close up and then she insists on driving me to her place. It reminds me of years gone by when we'd show up at one another's homes before a school dance or a date, borrowing clothes and doing one another's hair or makeup. That seems like ten lifetimes ago. I have a child, and my days of dating are light years behind me. But here we are.

Hannah pulls clothes out of her closet and throws them on the bed, holding them up to me one item at a time and making all sorts of expressions from approval to critique. She settles on a red sweater dress that does not leave any question as to whether I have the hips and chest of a woman who gave birth and nursed her child years ago. I tell her so and she laughs.

"If only we all could be so lucky to look like this after childbirth and motherhood has its way with us. You really don't know, do you?"

"Know what?" I ask as she zips up the back.

"How beautiful you are."

"I mean, I'm not ugly."

"Got that right. You're naturally gorgeous. And I won't say his name, but I think that tool of an ex of yours is still taking up real estate in your head. You should know how stunning you are. Men look at you, Heather."

"Floyd flirts, sure." I grin.

"That's just wrong on every level. I'm talking about men in your age-range, not men who could have parented your babysitters."

We both laugh.

"Well, I think I've turned off the part of my brain that has anything to do with attraction. It's self-preservation. And it's practical. I don't have time for men. So, I ignore them, unless they are ordering coffee. I'll pour them a cup, smile, and go on with my day."

"Ugh. I get it. But Heather, Floyd isn't wrong. We're only young once. You're an amazing mom. And you run that shop like a champ. But you deserve a life outside Cataloochee. Let loose tonight. Just for one night. Then you can put on that apron and get right back to ignoring the fine men of Henderson and Haywood counties. Heck, you can ignore all of North Carolina if you want."

"You say that now."

She smiles.

"Now. Sit down so I can do your face. And we're going to do something with that hair of yours too. Dry shampoo and some volumizing. Nothing radical. Just a little touch up to give it that special umph."

"I really don't want a special umph. I wouldn't know what to do with an umph, let alone a special one."

Hannah laughs. "You don't know what you want. Thankfully, I do."

An hour later I'm on my way up to my sister's house in Hannah's brown knee-high leather boots, a red sweater dress, makeup, and I'm sporting hair with umph. My cozy, ugly socks are screaming my name as I step out of my car and walk toward my sister's house.

This is absurd.

What am I doing?

I'm about to turn around and send Tasha a text saying I

got a last-minute headache when the front door swings open.

Rene is standing there and our eyes meet. And, oh my. He looks better than good in a hi-I'm-French-and I've-been-being-all-domestic-for-you way. I want to look away, because my whole body seems to be coming to life at the sight of him and the way he's looking at me.

"Wow."

He simply says that one word. But the way he says it makes it seem like he just read me a poem. His face is soft and kind, and his eyes say, *in another lifetime we'd make something beautiful together.*

Of all the things, Floyd's words about being young vaguely trickle through my mind. So I smile.

"Heather, ouah," Rene repeats, using a word that feels like *wow*, but it carries more heat when he says it in his native tongue. And then he's stepping out the door and walking toward me while I'm hoping I don't stumble and take a spill. When did it become a skill-test just to walk across a driveway?

This man never seems to hold back his real thoughts. At least I always know where he's coming from. Not much chance of him pulling a fast one on me if he's so transparent and forthcoming. It's refreshing, but also disarming. I'm not saying I don't like it. I just don't know what to do with him.

"Wow? Did you not expect me? Am I too early?"

I'm obviously trying to diffuse the situation and this unexpected electricity crackling between us.

"You are right on time. I meant, wow, as in, wow, you look stunning. So beautiful. You are always beautiful, but tonight ... well, tonight you look exceptional."

"Um. Thank you." I feel suddenly shy and unsteady.

"May I?" Rene extends his hand toward me as if he knows I'm the equivalent of a newborn baby giraffe. Sexy, I know. What can I say?

"I can walk myself to the door."

I stiffen a little, and I hate myself for being so stubborn and hard to reach. It's a knee-jerk reaction born of adversity. But I'm beyond tired of being the president and manager of Heather island, population of one.

"You can run a business and raise a child single-handedly." Rene smiles softly. "I'm quite sure you can make it across a driveway. I was offering because I need something to do with my hands after seeing you looking like that."

"Oh." *Oh.*

He looks at me so earnestly. His comment should feel inappropriate, but it's so plainly spoken it ends up being the best compliment of my life.

I should let Rene guide me across the pavement. There are a few scattered icy patches still left from our last storm. But I don't think I'd know what to do with my hands if he actually touched me after giving me that compliment, so I walk over to him, and in the most unusual gesture of my life, I lean in and air kiss each of Rene's cheeks. I'm so careful not to touch his skin, but I manage to blow kisses at the sides of his face, which seems like a safe compromise until I get a whiff of his cologne and something that smells like a home cooked meal, and another layer of scent that's sheer man. My eyes flutter shut before I have a chance to get a hold of myself, and in that moment, Rene leans in and brushes the softest kiss across the cheek nearest to him. His end-of-the-day scruff drags softly across my face as he pulls away and I shiver.

I don't make a little involuntary humming noise of appreciation. Nope. That would be embarrassing.

When I step back, Rene's got this grin on his face. It's not smug. But it's not exactly humble either.

He extends his arm again. "Shall we? Pierre and I made a chateaubriand with potatoes and vegetable confit."

"I have no idea what all that is, but I'm hungry, so ..."

Rene laughs like I told the funniest joke. The two of us walk toward the house like old friends, only friends that would like to see what it would be like to share a kiss that didn't land on a cheek. Rene gently takes my hand and wraps it around his forearm. His arm muscles are firm and he's warm, and I feel all sorts of things I shouldn't be feeling.

Just for tonight.

I can be a woman with her hand on a gorgeous man's amazing forearm. No problemo.

When I glance over at Rene, our faces are so close to one another he could lean right in and kiss me. He won't, and he doesn't. Which is good, obviously. He's just right there. And when his eyes meet mine, they crinkle around the edges with his smile. Everything this man does is riveting. And I feel like he intends that smile to be just for me, which is dangerous, but also thrilling.

Maybe it's the dress and the boots.

It's probably the special umph.

I laugh quietly to myself. I'm so out of my depth here.

I keep my mouth shut and thank my lucky stars when we make it in the front door and he lets my arm drop to my side. My sister comes through from the kitchen and her mouth pops open and then she lets out a whistle like she's a construction worker appreciating a woman walking by in a pencil skirt and stilettos.

The smell in this house is indescribable. It's beefy, and cozy, and delicious.

"What?" I ask Tasha, running my hand down the front of the dress.

"Wowzers, Heath. You look gorgeous. Doesn't she look beautiful?" she asks Rene, of all people.

"Oui. I already told her. Stunning. La plus belle femme que j'ai jamais vue."

My sister must have forgotten that I don't speak any French, unless you count saying *croissant* about twenty or thirty times a day.

"Est-ce ainsi?" she asks.

"Oui. Tellement vrai."

"Um. Someone translate, please."

"I will," Pierre sticks his head out from the kitchen. "My best friend said you are the most beautiful woman he's ever seen. Then my wife basically said, '*Really?*' and he said it's very true."

Pierre looks me over. "Second best." He gives a nod of finality, and then he disappears back into the kitchen.

Rene leans in toward me. "He has to say that or he'll be in trouble with your sister."

I giggle like a schoolgirl. *What has come over me?* You'd think I'd never seen a man before. Then again, Rene isn't just any man. If there's a more appealing man on the planet, I haven't met him. I had put him in a box, conveniently tucked away, and labeled it: *Men To Be Avoided Because They Are Entirely Too Flirtatious.* It's a long label, but it worked.

Over time, Rene has broken out of safekeeping and shown me he's not just another pretty face. Though he's definitely a pretty face.

Rene doesn't seem to mind my bumbling, nervous ways. He's still smiling softly at me.

"Can I get you a glass of wine or some cider? We are nearly ready to eat."

"I'll just have a drink with dinner."

"As you wish."

He keeps saying that. It's my favorite line from one of my most cherished books that was turned into a movie. I doubt Rene knows the movie. It's coincidence, but everytime he says it I melt a little inside. I've always wanted a man who would say those words and mean them. Unfortunately, this man is the wrong one for so many reasons.

Just for tonight.

Hannah seems to be cheering me on, if only in those three short words.

Pierre and Rene place the food onto plates in the kitchen and insist Tasha and I sit while they serve us. Besides Nate bringing me slightly-burnt toast and milk in bed on Mother's Day, I don't know when a man has served me food.

Dinner is far less uncomfortable than I had feared it would be. The food is incredible. I've eaten Pierre's cooking many times, but tonight's meal seems extra special. I want to think it's due to Rene's touch, and then I hope it's not. He's already making uninvited inroads into my heart.

My boots are kicked off and resting by the front door. There's a fire in the hearth. We're all laughing and talking comfortably. I haven't felt awkward since the first few minutes after Rene and I walked in together.

I'm avoiding being alone with my sister. She'll grill me about the outfit, makeup and hair. Then she'll want to play matchmaker and dream up some idyllic future where I marry her husband's best friend and we have dinners like this all the time.

Besides intentionally avoiding Tasha, I'm not even thinking about myself and how I look, even though Rene keeps staring at me with this expression I haven't seen in a man's eyes in years. It's expectant, but reserved. He's so focused on me, it should feel awkward, but instead I feel ... cherished. It's a heady experience to be on the receiving end of all that smolder and attention. And he gives it so freely and casually, but with such sincerity.

"So, Heather, what will you do with your shop now that those two have quit?" Rene studies me, his eyes lingering on my face as if we're the only two in the room. Then he takes a careful sip of his wine, swirling it with a practiced precision that seems like second nature. It's sexy and distracting.

I almost forget his question.

"Oh. It's not my shop. Cataloochee belongs to Melanie and Stan—an older couple in town. They are near retirement, though. So, they are thinking of selling."

"So you will buy it?" Rene asks.

"If only."

"If only, what?"

"I mean, I would love to. But I ... I'm not in a position."

Rene studies my face. His nod says everything his words never could.

"But if you had the money, you would buy the shop from them."

Direct and to the point as ever. I wonder if this man has any restraint. He says just what he's thinking without hesitation. My thoughts inconveniently drift to what a kiss from him would be like. If he's this direct about his thoughts and opinions, would he be that straightforward when kissing a woman?

I take a sip of my water and then I answer. "If I could, I would buy the shop—in a hot minute. Catty Coffee has been a haven for me during ... harder times. And I love serving the community. I adore everything about my job there. I had dreamed of owning the shop one day. But that doesn't look like it's in the cards, so I'm just hoping the new owners decide the space should remain a coffee shop, and that they're in the market to keep a manager on staff."

"They would be foolish to repurpose a business when it's thriving and the community loves it so much. If these new owners want a different type of shop, they should buy another space." He pauses and looks at me with that intense stare again. His gaze is thoughtful and makes me feel so seen. "That shop ... everything about it is very special—the kind of place you find once in your lifetime."

The way he says it, I almost believe he's talking about more than the shop now.

"Yes," I say. "But not everything special lasts."

"And not everything special ends either."

Rene picks my hand up off the table and kisses the back of it, just like that: his lips to my hand. His kiss doesn't linger. It's just a brush of his lips gently across my skin while his eyes hold mine. I feel that kiss everywhere. I'm stunned and overwhelmed and on fire. No biggie. Pay no attention to the woman who hasn't been kissed in five-plus years. Six? Who knows. All I do know is that Rene's kiss to the back of my hand was hotter than most kisses I've ever had anywhere over my entire lifetime.

Rene gently places my hand back on the table as if he hadn't just rocked my world.

He doesn't know, and that's all for the better.

Pierre clears his throat. "Rene, help me with dessert, s'il vous plaît."

"Of course." Rene turns to me. "Don't go anywhere, Cher. The dessert is always the best part."

Pierre and Rene take the dirty dishes and disappear into the kitchen.

And then I'm alone in the dining room with my younger sister.

9

RENE

And some kind of help is the kind of help.
We all can do without.
~ Shel Silverstein

"Un baiser à la main?" Pierre gives me a scolding glance as soon as we walk into the kitchen, leaving Heather and Tasha alone at the dining table together.

Pierre's voice is low and private. He adds a tsk, tsk, for good measure.

I set the dinner dishes in the sink while he removes the dessert from the warming oven.

"Oui. I kissed her hand. It's not what you think."

"Oh, edify me as to how that was not you being overly sensual with a vulnerable woman. I know what my eyes saw. And the way she looked after you set her hand down ..."

"How did she look?" *Was she affected by my gesture? Because, unfortunately, I was.*

I felt as if the table had shrunk to seat only two, and the world had gone still. Heather and I were there, alone, bantering lightly, exchanging veiled comments about love and the possibilities for her future if she would only open her heart again.

I heard nothing but her words. I saw nothing but her beauty. I felt nothing but her indecision and that ever-present fire beneath the surface. Tonight, she is a woman who needs to be noticed—to be the sole focus of a man's appreciation and respect. And she had mine from the moment I opened the door to greet her in the driveway. That red dress might be the death of me. In another lifetime, I'd be the man pursuing her.

Pierre's brows draw together. His lips thin. His voice nears a whisper, but his words are more clipped than usual. "I told you she is not in a position to date or to be the temporary recipient of your charm."

My volume matches Pierre's. "That is where you are wrong. Have a little faith in me! Do you really think I would take advantage of Heather? Especially on a night when her employees left her more stressed than before? I see her. Heather needs to be pushed out of her resignation. She is still a young woman. She is beautiful, and she has a sharp wit and a warm heart. A man would be lucky to catch her—to be the one she finally chooses to give herself a second chance at love with. But she doesn't know herself—she only sees a compartmentalized version of who she truly is. She needs to remember that she's a woman."

"And you are the man to remind her?"

"Not in the way you think. I am here, and then I will go

home. Heather and I are intertwined because you and Tasha are forever connected. I would be a fool to pursue her. But I'm just the man to help her remember what is possible, and to gently shake her out of her determination to face life alone because one man couldn't see the treasure he had in her. Trust me, mon ami, I'm not here to do harm. I'm being careful with her heart."

Pierre snorts. Not like a pig. It's a sound we make in France—a combination of a short hum at the back of the throat and some noise we make through our nose when we feel skeptical.

"You will see. I am the most careful man you know." I tiptoe around the kitchen. "See. This is her heart." I point to the floor in the center of the room. "And this is me." I point to myself as I tiptoe all around the area that is Heather's heart. "So careful. Never stepping where I don't belong."

Pierre chuckles. "Why do I miss you, even now? You are here. And you are as much of a pain as ever."

"I miss you too," I admit, though he knows it. "You never were enough of a pain. Boring yes. Très très boring! It's nearly a sleep aid when I think of how unpainful you were."

We share a laugh and then we embrace like brothers. Pierre claps me on my shoulders when we separate. He carries the galette into the dining area and I follow behind him with a stack of dessert plates.

"Dessert is served," he announces.

Heather smiles at me. "Did you bake this too?"

"I sliced the apples and seasoned them with cinnamon and other spices and sugar. I hope it is to your liking."

"It beats canned soup." Her eyes hold mine and we share a private smile.

"You're welcome here any night Nate is with Mom and

Dad," Tasha says. "You know you don't have to stay home and eat soup."

"I don't mind my nights alone. I've grown accustomed to them. They're a reminder of my life and how it will be when Nate moves on."

"Ahh. It won't be that way then," I assure her.

I lift one of the plates and place a slice of the galette on it. Then I set the plate in front of Heather.

"What do you mean?" Tasha asks, reminding me instantly that Heather and I are not alone.

I don't look at Pierre. He's made his point, and I'm making mine.

"I mean," I look at Tasha instead of Heather. "Your sister assumes she will be alone when Nate is ready to launch into his young adult life. I highly doubt she will be alone. She has far too much to offer. Some man will come along and steal her heart. She will not be in ugly socks eating soup out of a can unless she is sitting next to the man wearing matching socks and holding another bowl of the same soup."

I slice another piece of the tart and put it on a plate to pass to Tasha.

Heather makes a sound like *hmph*. But Tasha jumps on my idea like a campaign manager on the trail to gather voter support.

"You are so right! I keep telling her she's not going to be single forever."

"Next subject," Heather says.

I glance at Pierre. He nods in agreement with Heather.

"Okay. Next subject," I agree.

Heather looks at Tasha. "I have a big favor to ask you."

"Anything."

"Nate needs to come here tomorrow while I wrap up

work. On school days I'm going to try to see if I can get someone to cover the morning hour I take him to school—just like Jessa did. And usually he can just come to Catty after school until I close. But tomorrow I have the town council in there all afternoon and I would rather if Nate weren't underfoot. He gets a little intrusive."

Tasha says, "Nate for mayor!"

"I could see that one day," I add.

Then Tasha puts her hand over Heather's. "I'll be in during the morning shift once this recording gig is over. Next week, for sure. And Nate can come here tomorrow, or any day. But I can't pick him up either of the next two days because I'm in Asheville."

"I know. Don't worry. I'll work it out." Heather's spine stiffens.

Over the course of dinner, I watched her relax more and more. Now she is back into business mode.

Before anyone can say another word, I speak up. "I can come in the next two mornings this week. And I'll also pick Nate up from his school tomorrow if that would help. You'll just have to tell me where it is. If Pierre can loan me the car again, I'll do what's needed."

"Oh! You don't have to. You're here on vacation."

"I'm here to ... see my friends."

I don't explain to Heather that I'm here to sort out my own mind, or any of the other myriad of things I've realized since coming to America.

"I can help you and Nate. It will keep me from being bored, and it will keep me out of trouble."

"I doubt that," my best friend mutters from across the table.

I smile at him and wink.

"For tomorrow, if you would, that would be great." Heather's voice is soft.

"I would love to. Tomorrow and Friday. Let me do this one thing for you."

"If I don't have anyone on shift by Friday, I'll let you know. And your croissant and espresso are on the house."

"I accept."

It's obvious Heather doesn't want to be the person desperately needing others to pitch in and give of their time and effort. That's exactly why I'm so adamant about contributing to what she needs. I've got a little over two weeks to help her see that she can trust a man again and let someone eventually love her. I can't really say why this matters so much to me. Maybe I'm a man who likes projects —to feel I'm being useful and making a difference in someone's life. I know it's more than that when I look up and see Heather's soft eyes studying my face like I'm a puzzle.

* * *

The next morning my alarm goes off at four in the morning. Thankfully, my body is still confused and easily wakes at what would be ten in France. I quietly move through my room, changing into clothes. Once I'm dressed, I grab the keys Pierre reluctantly left out for me on the counter. He thanked me for pitching in and then couldn't help himself by adding another admonishment about Heather's vulnerability. He suggested I go out with someone else while I'm here if I'm so desperate for female attention. He means well.

And it is not like Pierre's concerns are unfounded. I have spent many of my adult years surrounded by females and purposely remaining unattached. Pierre has no idea the depth of my thoughts about my life these days. We haven't made the time to connect at that level on this visit yet. And even if I do share with him, Pierre is the type who will believe what he sees over any profession I make about going through a change. And he will see. I will show him.

The cold air chills my cheeks as I walk to the car. I'll have coffee at the shop. And then I'll bring Nate back here this afternoon. Who knows what he and I will do to occupy ourselves. At least Pierre will be here too, though he's getting a head start on his next novel since inspiration hit him. Pierre's far more diligent than most workers who have designated hours and a place to be every day. I relate to being my own demanding boss. No one expects more of me than I do.

I pull into a spot down the block from Cataloochee, leaving the diagonal spaces in front of the shop wide open for customers who will be here in fewer than two hours. When I open the shop door, expecting to see Heather— maybe even anticipating the sight of her in a way that I will examine later—I am shocked to see her mother instead.

"Oh! Bonjour!" I call out. "Good morning, Louisa."

"Rene. It's so good you came. What a sweet gesture. Heather's in the back doing something or other. And I'm just here ... tidying things up."

"I'm glad to help. You are Pierre's family. And Pierre is like a brother to me, so ..."

"Well, I'm so glad you consider us family. To think, I have French relatives. I never imagined."

Finally, an American woman who appreciates what it means to be French.

"I'll just go see what Heather wants me to do," I say, walking past her mother into the back.

Louisa's prediction follows me through the swinging door. "She probably won't let you do a thing."

"Bonjour, belle femme," I greet Heather. "I'm here to help. Put me to work."

She looks far more casual than she did last night. An image of her in that dress and those boots flashes in my mind and I smile at the memory. Every version of Heather is beautiful, though. Dressed up, or like this—in her T-shirt, jeans and tennis shoes with her hair pulled back from her face in a ponytail.

Heather looks up from a paper she's holding. "Oh. Hi. Good morning."

She doesn't acknowledge that I called her beautiful. Probably for the best. She's here at work, and we need to focus on preparing for the day. When she's more at ease, I will make sure she receives my compliments.

"Could you take my mom home?" She looks serious.

"Does she need a ride home?"

"No. But she's basically talking about redecorating the shop. And she thinks she can make coffee. Which she can ... at home. But here ... it's all different. And she brought paint."

Her voice is rapid and wobbly.

And ... *paint*?

I don't think. On instinct, I step closer to Heather. "Cher." I clasp both her shoulders with my hands and look down into her eyes. Surprisingly, she doesn't back away or shrug my hands loose. "You will be okay. The shop will be fine. Your customers love you. You have earned that. And each of them would make their own coffee or clear plates or do whatever you needed to keep the morning running smoothly and to share your burden this week. Take a breath. I'll go handle your mother."

She smiles up at me. "Thank you."

I feel my face soften and then it's as though I suddenly realize how near I am to her with my hands on her arms. I step backward.

"Okay." Heather blows out a breath. "Let's do this."

I smile at her. She is so strong. What a woman.

When I walk out from the kitchen, Heather's mother has an assortment of employee name tags lined up on the counter, along with what appears to be bottles of craft paint.

"What do we have here?" I ask as casually as possible, and in a tone I hope doesn't alert Heather.

"I'm spiffing up the nametags."

"Spiffing?" I'm relatively fluent in English, but some vernacular flies over my head.

"Making them more appealing. They're so bland now. They need character."

I clear my throat. I deal with tricky personalities all day selling properties. "Is this something Heather wanted you to do?"

Louisa looks at me for a moment. Then, by some miracle, she seems to realize Heather may not be in favor of a pre-dawn paint project on the nametags.

"I'll just check with her," Louisa says.

"I'll start the coffee."

"You can do that?"

"Oui. It's one of my few talents on earth. But I manage somehow."

Louisa laughs lightly. "You're funny. You know that?"

"Thank you."

I get to work going through the steps Heather showed me to make the coffee for the morning. Then I check the pastry display. I don't really know what else to do.

Louisa comes back out, looking a little like a child

resisting naptime. "I'm supposed to do this in the office and only for the employees who work full time, and not for Heather. Which only leaves you and me."

I smile. "Well, I'll look forward to whatever you make me. Though, I'm not sure how long your daughter will allow me to contribute here."

"You still need a tag."

I nod and Louisa walks into the back, carrying our two name tags and her paint bottles and brushes.

Heather emerges a few moments later. "Why did I say yes to her helping?" She shakes her head. "Actually, I didn't! She just announced she was coming. I said it wasn't necessary. And then she just showed up."

"She won't do any harm in the office."

"True." She smiles a thin smile. "Although, you never know. If she starts organizing files ... Oh. You started the coffee. Tell me it was you and not my mom."

"It was me."

"Thank you."

Deliveries arrive, we stock cabinets and the back refrigerator. Heather grinds espresso beans and turns on the registers. A few minutes before six, customers start to gather outside the front door. Heather opens the shop for them with a smile.

I take orders for the next three hours, fulfilling basic requests for baked goods or coffee, while Heather mans the espresso machine. Her mom is in charge of clearing plates and she's given herself the job of chatting with everyone who comes in. Thankfully, Louisa also volunteers to go to Heather's home to wake Nate and take him to school so Heather can stay at the shop.

The only mishap of the morning comes when Louisa decides to make a smoothie for someone she knows. She's talking and dropping ingredients into the blender. Everything seems normal, except the crunching sound. I almost ask about it, but I assume it's the ice being incorporated into the drink.

When she opens the lid, she looks down into the concoction, smiles, and begins to pour the fruity drink into a tall to-go cup. A spoon comes sliding out, splattering smoothie across the counter, and all over Louisa's shirt and half-apron.

"Oh! That's what that noise was!" she exclaims.

But she still puts a lid on the drink and hands it to her friend who takes it with a smile. Then she wipes up and tosses the spoon in the trash without another word.

Neither of us says anything to Heather. I will—later. There's no need to disrupt her already scattered morning with blender mishaps.

By nine, the crowd has thinned. Heather is in the back working on some paperwork in the office.

My phone rings, and since we're in a lull, I answer. It's Tasha.

"Allo?"

"Hi, Rene. I started feeling badly that you're spending your holiday working for my sister for free, so I reached out to my friend Britt, the one I told you about, the realtor. She's free this afternoon to take you around town to see some homes for sale. She'll take you wherever you like, really. She's looking forward to meeting you. She also travels a lot. She's been all over Europe. Oh! And she speaks French."

"Sounds ... great. Thank you. But what about Nate?"

"Well, Pierre will get him. We'd handle this if you were overseas, you know. We're grateful for your kindness, but we don't want to impose. You're here to relax. Maybe have some fun. Right?"

"Sure. Yes. That's right."

"Great. Britt will meet you here at the house after lunch, unless you are staying in town for the rest of the morning."

Does Heather need me? It seems the biggest rush of the day is behind us.

Normally, the idea of spending time with a woman like the one Tasha is describing would make me eager to leave the coffee shop to get out and see the housing market, or just to spend the day with someone local. Right now, I feel like I'm letting Heather and Nate down somehow. Is it odd that I'd rather stay here at Catty Coffee? Perhaps it's the lure of the familiar. I've spent more time here than anywhere besides Pierre and Tasha's since coming back to Harvest Hollow.

When Heather comes back out front, she smiles at me and thanks me again. "I don't know what I would have done without you."

"Someone else would have filled the spot. You have many people who care and are willing."

"Maybe."

"What about the owners?"

Heather is bearing the weight of this business as if she owns it. Where are the people who have the biggest stake in this shop? Why aren't they stressing over hiring replacements, and manning the counter, and covering the time each morning when Heather needs to leave to wake her son and send him to school?

"I ... haven't exactly mentioned that Cedar and Jessa quit."

"You didn't tell them?"

"I don't want to worry Stan and Melanie. I want to handle things here. They count on me. If I run to them with this kind of situation instead of managing the details myself, they may not think I'm up to the task. I need this job."

"Of course."

I have a myriad of thoughts about Heather's stance, but it's not my place to express them.

"Your sister called. Apparently she's arranged for a friend to tour me around town. And she said Pierre will pick Nate up from school this afternoon."

"Oh. Okay. Well, that's great. You should enjoy your time off." Heather grabs a towel and starts wiping down the counters I just finished wiping. "Did she mention who was taking you on a tour?"

"Britt?"

"Oh. Great. Good. Britt's really sweet—and pretty. I think she might even speak French. She's been everywhere."

"That's what Tasha said."

Everything except saying Britt is pretty. That fact should make me all the more eager to meet her. I feel nothing but a strange obligation to be here at Cataloochee to support Heather.

"Okay. Well, have a great time."

Heather turns and walks into the back room without another word. I follow her, slightly confused at her reaction. Did she want me to stay and help?

"Heather?"

She's speed walking toward the office.

She slows and turns to look at me. "Yeah?"

"Did you need me to stay? This tour isn't important. I think Tasha is just trying to give me something to do."

Pierre's comments about Tasha's ulterior motives come to mind, but I keep those to myself.

"It will be fine," Heather smiles, but it's not full or relaxed. "Today's biggest rush is over. And I just had an answer to the ad I placed in the Harvest Times. I may have a new employee starting soon."

"That's great news."

"Yes. It is. Don't worry about us, Rene. We'll be fine. Go have fun. You can actually leave now. I can manage alone."

Those words feel like they allude to more than this temporarily short-staffed day at the shop. I thought I could manage alone too. And I have. I just don't think I want to anymore.

Heather changes directions and heads back out into the shop, brushing by me as she goes. The urge to reach out to her is strong and strange. We do have a history, but not an intimate one. If anything, Heather has scrutinized me and found me lacking each time I visited. I know she had assumed I'm careless in my relationships with women because I flirt and joke around. Regardless, the familiarity between us blurs lines. That doesn't explain the urge I have to gather Heather into my arms, or to take her away so we could spend an afternoon, just the two of us, talking and laughing. The image in my head feels too real, and it never will come to pass.

Maybe this day around town with Tasha's friend, Britt, is just the distraction I need. A little space apart will clear my head.

I follow Heather into the main shop and grab my coat off the hook on the wall behind the counter.

"I'll see you tomorrow morning."

"Have a good day, Rene."

Heather doesn't tell me not to bother coming in tomorrow. I smile as I walk into the cold morning air.

10

HEATHER

Practical people would be more practical
if they would take a little more time for dreaming.

~ J. P. McEvoy

I lock the shop behind me and walk to my car. As far as insane days go, this one wasn't too bad. Mom confessed the blender mishap before she left. It still seems to run fine, so I don't have to go to Stan and Melanie about a thousand dollar equipment replacement.

The interior of the car is chilly. I turn the heat on high as I make my way out of town toward my sister's. Pierre picked Nate up from school, so I'll be picking him up there and bringing him home for dinner and bed. And then I'll collapse—finally.

The best part of my day happened when I interviewed a college student named Simon. I'm thinking the fact that he's not named after any natural element could possibly mean he won't abandon me to go hiking anytime soon. My new interview question includes, "How many weeks' notice would you give me if you had to quit?" Simon answered with, "at least two." I basically decided to hire him on the spot after that answer. Besides, he has experience as a barista in Boston, where he lived the past few years before moving to Harvest Hollow when his girlfriend relocated.

I pull my car into Tasha and Pierre's driveway. When I step out of the driver's seat, I can't help remembering the look on Rene's face when he opened the door last night and saw me. Or the way he smelled. Or the feel of his lips on my hand. Or his kind words. But he spent the day with Britt, a successful, beautiful, well-traveled single woman. Britt's Tasha's age, and she also does not have an eight-year-old or a freight train's worth of personal baggage from a failed marriage.

When I open my sister's front door and shout, "Hey, honey, I'm home!" my words nearly get stuck in my mouth. I didn't expect to see what I'm looking at.

Rene is sitting cross-legged on the floor across from Nate. They both are holding a hand of Uno cards and they have what I would call their *game faces* on.

"Oh hi, Mom," Nate says without even turning to look at me. "Wait a minute. I still need to win this round."

"Hello, Heather," Pierre says. He glances away from his computer only for the briefest moment to smile at me.

Rene looks up at me and smiles a smile that makes me feel like I'm still wearing Hannah's sweater dress. I know what I look like after a full day at Catty. I have the sudden urge to run into the hall bathroom to freshen up.

"Listen to this, Mom!" Nate says in a voice that's too loud, but it's his default setting.

"What's that, Nater Potater?"

I'm still standing in the doorway, frozen in place and unsure where I fit into this configuration. Pierre is typing away on his laptop on the couch, already oblivious to his surroundings again, as he always is when he's writing.

"Say it, Mister Rene!" Nate commands.

Rene catches my eyes again and says, "That's a total W, bae."

His French accent makes the sentence sound even more out of place than it would if he were American.

I smile. The way Rene's looking at me feels like he's saying something far more sultry and intimate than the ridiculous phrase my son obviously taught him. But I laugh anyway.

"Do another one!" Nate commands.

"Slaayyy, bro."

Rene looks at Nate for his approval and Nate beams over at him with a look I don't think I've ever seen him give another adult.

"Did you just say, 'Slay, bro?'" I ask, unable to hide my amusement.

This. This is what it would be like to come home to a man who loved my son. I've had the blessing of Pierre stepping in. My dad fills his role as grandpa. But nothing has felt so heart-stoppingly close to what I dared not long for until I opened the door tonight.

"Oui, Cher. I said, 'Slay, bro.'" Rene wags his eyebrows like he just learned the innermost secrets to our language. "Your son is teaching me all the things I didn't know to say in English."

I shake my head, laughing at the idea of Rene trying to

use any of these phrases again anywhere else outside this room.

"No. Just no." I can't help laughing. "It's awful. That's not ... just ... don't."

"What, Mom? He might need to know some things."

"Come in, Cher." Rene tips his chin toward me in a beckoning gesture. "We are only finishing one more hand of this game. We have a bet, so I can't give up now."

"A bet?"

I walk toward the couch and take a seat on the edge of the last cushion. Pierre is on the other end from me, still absorbed in whatever he's creating.

"Oui. If Nate wins, I have to take him out to ice cream."

"And if you win?"

"If I win, Nate will learn to speak some French."

"Hmmm." I hum. "I don't think my son loses on this one either way."

"Well, you are right, of course. But he was not thrilled about the idea of learning a language, even if it is French. So, I asked him to teach me some of the English I do not yet know. And he did, as you can see."

"Yes. He most certainly did." I laugh. It's an uncharacteristic sound, like I'm a high school girl and the captain of the football team stopped to ask me for my number.

Only, Rene spent the day with Britt. And he's going back to France in two weeks.

Pierre looks up, stares at me, then Rene, then back at me. His face looks pensive, brows drawn in, mouth thinly pressed into a line. Maybe he's planning this next book and he's stuck in his process.

Rene smiles his trademark carefree grin at Pierre and then looks back at me. "What are you doing tonight?"

"Tonight?"

"Yes. You've had a long day. What are you doing now?"

"Going home. Probably picking up pizza ..."

I don't finish my sentence because my sister comes through the door.

"Hey, everyone! We're home!"

She refers to herself as *we* now that she's pregnant. It's pretty adorable.

"Welcome home, Cher," Pierre sets his laptop down. All previous dour expressions seem to be out the window as he strides towards his wife like a man who hasn't seen the woman he loves in months, not hours.

"Awww. You missed me," Tasha coos.

"I did. Very much."

They embrace and kiss in a way that makes me want to cover my son's eyes. But I don't have to because Nate shouts, "Gross!" causing my sister and her affectionate husband to separate.

Rene is laughing on the other side of the coffee table from me, but when he looks at me, there's a heat to his expression. If I were a dreamer, I'd say he was telling me he'd kiss me like that if I'd let him. Which I won't, so the point is absurd. Still, I feel the blush creep up my neck.

I stand quickly. "Okay, Nater. Let's hit the road."

"Awwww ..." he whines, like every child his age when told to pack it up and get ready to go.

"Was someone talking about pizza?" Tasha asks from the doorway where Pierre is helping her out of her coat and taking her bags from her.

"I just told Rene that Nate and I would pick some pizza up on our way back to our place."

"Why don't you just stay here. We can order pizza in ... and play Uno. Looks like they already started."

"Oui. But this Uno takes bets," Rene says.

"Bets? I'm in!" Tasha looks at me with that younger sister pleading look she's used all her life to get her way.

"Okay. We'll stay. But I have to get Nate home in two hours. It's a school night."

"Yay!" Nate shouts.

"Slay, bae!" Rene shouts after him.

And the whole room erupts in laughter.

11

RENE

Sometimes all you need is one person that shows you that it's okay to let your guard down, be yourself, and love with no regrets.

~ Unknown

"So, how did your tour of Harvest Hollow with Britt go?" Heather asks me as we're cleaning up from the morning rush.

I tell myself the slight clip in her voice means she might be jealous. I'm wise enough to know she's not, but a man can dream.

It has been five days since Britt tried to take me out for the afternoon. That was the same day Heather and Nate stayed for pizza and Uno at Pierre and Tasha's. We all ate sitting on the floor around the coffee table. It was the most casual meal I've ever enjoyed. But best of all was the way

Heather relaxed. She smiled and laughed freely, seeming to forget herself and the stress of running the shop for a while.

I came in and helped her the following morning. I had said I would, and she hadn't told me not to, so I kept my word.

When I showed up Saturday without any warning, she looked surprised, but she didn't tell me to go home, so I put on an apron and the very colorful name tag Louisa had made for me. It has a pink Eiffel Tower, a yellow macaroon, and a long tan object that I think is supposed to be a baguette scattered around my name in a very flourishing font.

Pierre came in on Saturday and had his fun commenting on it. I wear the name tag proudly. It's a conversation piece. And it means I have a place here, even if I am an uninvited volunteer. By Sunday morning, when I showed up, Heather had already set out a small cup filled with two steaming shots of espresso, freshly brewed for me and sitting next to a plate with a croissant. Her anticipation of my arrival made me smile.

Now it's Monday and we have our rhythm for the morning routine down like a science. Only there's a new hire here—Simon. He can't keep his eyes off Heather, but he's a hard worker, and he seems to know what he's doing. He's obviously too young for Heather, and she's obviously oblivious to the way he stares at her with hearts in his eyes wherever she goes. I am not so sure I appear much different. The more time I spend with Heather, the less interest I have in preparing her heart for another man. I find myself imagining I'm that man, even if the reality of our situation is that I won't be here in ten days. And her sister is still my best friend's wife. We wouldn't get a second chance if we mess things up.

I lean back on the wall, watching Heather as she rearranges the remaining pastries in the case. She's bent over, busying herself. I have to study the chalkboard with our specials on it so I don't stand here staring.

"It was not exactly a tour. Britt showed up to take me around to see some homes, but before we even made it to the first one, she got a call to show a home to a young couple, so she had to turn around and take me back to Pierre's. That's why I ended up being the one to pick Nate up from school, and then I spent the afternoon learning how to play Uno—a game I lost every time. I still owe Nate an ice cream. I hope to settle that debt this afternoon."

"*You* picked Nate up that day?"

She stands and looks me in the eye.

"I did. Pierre was so focused on plotting his next novel and I was not doing anything important, so I went. I hope that's okay."

"It's ... great. Thank you."

"It was my pleasure. He's a wonderful boy."

Heather smiles a full smile. "He's pretty obsessed with you now."

"Is he? I seem to have that effect on most people."

"Do you? I hadn't noticed."

"I said, most."

"I haven't met many who weren't taken in by your charm."

"Is it still charm if it's sincere?"

"I think it's all the more dangerous when it's sincere."

I push off the wall, walking toward her. The shop is empty except for a businessman who is immersed in his laptop and another young woman wearing a pair of headphones and keeping her face buried in a book. She's separated from anything going on around her. Simon is in the back, on dish duty.

I stand directly in front of Heather, grabbing the towel that's sitting next to the register as if that's why I've walked over here. "You keep calling me dangerous, Cher."

She flushes slightly. "You are."

"Dangerous to whom? I promise I am as harmless, playful and affectionate as a kitten."

"Kittens can destroy your furniture, stink up your house, and scratch you when they only mean to be playful."

"Ouch." I smile at her. "I promise I won't ruin your furniture. I don't stink." I smell under my armpit to prove the point, and to make her laugh. I love that laugh. She rewards me by breaking into a smile and adding the giggle I seem to be responsible for dragging out of her regularly these days. I've never heard her laugh with that same laughter for anyone else. "And I will never scratch you, Cher." I wink.

This is the closest I've ever come to saying what I really feel and think about her, though, she must have some suspicion. We are not children or young adults in our early twenties. She has been married. I've dated many women. We've lived enough life to know what we do and don't want in a romantic involvement. Heather is everything I would want if our circumstances were different.

She and I can't pursue anything serious, but maybe we could have a date. And then I will take my heart back to France where I will cherish whatever we shared and release the hope of more with her—eventually, over time.

Heather shakes her head lightly, smiles a shy smile at me, and then grabs the coffee pot to fill the cups of the two customers who have long since neglected their mugs for whatever they are reading or typing.

We dance around one another the rest of the morning, casting sidelong glances at one another and giving each other private smiles. It's like looking in the window of a confectioner's shop but finding the door locked. The experience is both tempting and frustrating. Mostly, though, I am watching Heather thaw in front of me. Over a week ago, she avoided my eyes, kept her distance, and put up invisible barriers. Now she accepts my flirting and even rewards me in the form of her smiles and giggles. I notice that look in her eyes—the one that tells me she feels this too—at least I hope she does.

Pierre arrives just before lunch. He's made progress plotting his novel and, according to him, feels like the world's worst friend for neglecting me while I visit.

We leave Catty together to take a hike in the local hills. Pierre drives through town and then out to a small parking lot with a trailhead leading into the woods.

"I apologize again for my neglect."

"I understand. This trip was not planned. You have a life here. Your work has its demands."

"No. That all is true, but I should have been more attentive to you. Instead, I've left you to fend for yourself and spend your days working as a helper to my sister-in-law."

"That has been no hardship. I, strangely, enjoy being at Catty Coffee."

"Ahh. So now you call it Catty?"

"It is the name most of the locals use."

"And you know what this means?"

"Nothing?"

"No. It means you are falling under the spell of Harvest Hollow." He glances over at me with a grin.

I step up over a root and continue to walk the narrow dirt trail surrounded by trees and low brush. It feels good to be out in nature, breathing the cool air, stretching my muscles.

"Soon you will tell time by the clock tower. You will plan a night at one of our best restaurants, Harvested, to celebrate special occasions. When you are in town, you will stop at the General Store to pick up the silliest items, always pausing to talk to Mel on your way out. You will get your books at Book Smart, and the rest you will borrow from the town library. And every weekend, you will look forward to the seasonal farmers market so you can find the freshest ingredients for your meals."

I am ahead of Pierre by a few steps on the trail as it winds upward to the spot where it appears to level out. I turn to look at him over my shoulder.

"It all starts with this: calling the coffee shop Catty. You, my friend, are falling for this town. And I'm wondering if you even know it."

"Ridicule!" I nearly shout the word in French. I follow it with, "Absurde!" for good measure. "I enjoy this town as any man enjoys his vacation. But a vacation is not a life. And a town you visit is not your home. My home is in Avignon. Not all of us are able to leave so easily."

"I did not leave easily." Pierre's voice is soft.

"Je suis désolé. I am sorry. I know you did not. And how could you not move where the woman who captured your heart lives? Her family is here. She needs you to be here. I see it now. And I was the one who pushed you into this, asked you to see what you could not. So, am I not to blame?"

"There is no blame for a happy decision. The only downfall is the separation from you—and my family, of course."

"A high price indeed. No one should be so far from me. It's tragic to live a Rene-free existence." I smile and Pierre chuckles.

"The highest price, to be sure." Pierre's voice is sincere.

The trail levels out and we suddenly have a breathtaking view that nearly makes me gasp. Mountains spread to all sides of us, valleys and hills as far as the eye can see.

I stand still, admiring the beauty.

"Ah, oui. We also have this." Pierre winks. "You should see it in the fall."

"You have many beautiful things here to tempt a man." I am not speaking of the mountains anymore. Pierre does not know, and he would chide me again if he did, but the mountains pale in comparison to his sister-in-law.

We walk an hour, saying little at times, and then talking comfortably about our lives. When we return to the car, I am restored. Perhaps I should visit Harvest Hollow a few times a year. I would be able to see Pierre's new baby, since I am unofficially the uncle. I could visit Heather. And what would that be like? She might find someone to trust—even to fall in love with. And then each visit would be the worst kind of torture, watching her unfurl for another man like a flower in the sunshine.

Pierre said I am falling for this town. He is wrong about the town, maybe not so far off about the falling.

Pierre drops me off in front of Catty Coffee when our hike is over. He's going to work some more on developing his story. I would rather be here. Maybe Heather needs some afternoon help. I carry my satchel with the book about the local actor tucked inside. If she doesn't need me, I will read.

I walk in and our eyes meet. She smiles over at me. I wink. Of course I do. Maybe I am a hopeless flirt. Maybe it's just the effect Heather has on me.

She finishes checking on the few customers scattered at tables around the shop, and then she joins me near my couch—which has been neglected by me over the past five days. But I have been happier by Heather's side than I was when I watched her from the safe comfort of this sofa.

"You're back."

"I am. The walk was très magnifique."

"I know that one. Very beautiful."

"You should know it."

She smiles, maybe because she can discern what I'm not saying.

"I'm here to help if you need me."

Heather looks around the shop. "It's pretty dead in here right now. I think I've got this."

"That was never a question," I assure her.

She smiles again and I collect her smiles like pennies in a jar, adding up to an unforeseen wealth.

"So, now that you have a free afternoon, what will you do with yourself?"

"I will sit there." I point to the couch. "And read my book."

"You need to get out more."

"I am out. My home is four thousand, five hundred miles away. I am very out."

She shakes her head. Then her brow furrows. "That's how far it is?"

"Yes. That is the distance between us."

"The distance between us," she echoes, thoughtfully.

It is—an insurmountable distance. But she is here now.

The urge to ask her on a date presses on me more strongly than ever.

The door opens. Nate flies through. That boy never walks. He is like a learjet appearing from nowhere at mach speed and skidding to a halt.

"Hi, Mister Rene! Is today ice cream day?"

"Homework first," Heather says.

"Okay, Mahhhm." Nate rolls his eyes.

I stifle a smile.

"Can I work out here?"

"You could sit with me." I point to the couch again, realizing I should lay claim to it now while it is still available. "I'll be reading over there."

"Reading? You aren't even in school."

"I know. It's crazy. But I still read even though no one forces me anymore."

"Gross." Nate dashes to the couch and starts to unzip his backpack.

"Let me know when you want to take him. I'll check his homework first," Heather says.

"Of course."

The door opens again and I start to wonder if Heather will need my help after all. A gentleman walks in, looking professional in pressed slacks, an oxford shirt and a tweed coat. His eyes land on Heather. I feel the urge to wrap my arm around her in a move that would stake my claim. Heather has become a friend. But she's not mine to hold or cherish. I have no right to these possessive feelings surging through me like a shot of adrenaline.

Heather sees the man too. She walks hurriedly over to the couch. "Nate, your customer is here. Help him while I just ... get some things in the storeroom."

"Really?" Nate's face is alight with excitement.

"Yep." Heather walks quickly away from Nate, never looking at the gentleman again. Is he her ex? No. Nate would know his own father. She is acting as though they have a history—one she wants to run from.

As she passes me, she quickly whispers, "Please watch Nate while he serves Brennan."

I nod, but I don't think she even registers my answer because she is moving toward the kitchen more quickly than I've ever seen her move.

Nate stands from the couch and addresses the man. "I think you get a Danish."

"I ... what?"

"My mom said you get a Danish when you come in. You're here for more than coffee, right?"

Ahhh. *This man.* The one Louisa sent to ask Heather out. I smile at the predicament unfolding in front of me. I'll keep an eye on Nate, but he doesn't seem to need my help. He's doing a great job chasing this man off.

"I get to serve you." Nate continues. "Do you want one?"

"A Danish?"

"Yeah." Nate looks about ready to give up on his opportunity to play storekeeper.

I take a seat on the couch, so glad I decided to come back here this afternoon. I would have hated to miss this. Not that I would want to be anywhere else.

"Sure. Nathan, is it?"

"It's Nate. Or Nate the Great. Or Nater Potater. *Not* Nathan."

Way to blow it with her son. I nearly chuckle.

"Follow me," Nate says.

The man does as he's told. His eyes rove the room and

land on the door leading to the kitchen. Heather hasn't returned from her speedy exit.

I watch from the couch as Nate picks up the tongs, asks the man what he wants, puts it in a bag, and takes the man's money. Nate never touches the register. He just puts the money on the rear counter near the espresso machine.

"I'll let my mom put that away. Are you supposed to get change?"

"Keep it. And my name is Brennan, Nate."

"Okay."

"It was good to meet you."

"Okay. Well, I gotta work on my homework. I'm getting ice cream. See ya."

Nate leaves the man standing at the counter, holding a paper bag with a Danish he probably didn't want. Nate joins me on the sofa.

"Was that fun?" I ask.

"Nah."

"Okay." I chuckle and lift my book.

The man, Brennan, stands at the counter a little longer and then leaves a few moments later, a dazed and disappointed look on his face.

Heather peers out from the kitchen less than a minute after Brennan leaves.

I raise my voice and say, "Coast is clear."

She lifts a finger to her mouth telling me to be quiet.

Something in me clicks when she smiles an embarrassed smile my way. She's looking adorable as ever, conspiring with me over this man she chased away. *I will ask her out.* We can spend time together, just two friends. Heather deserves a night out with a man who doesn't call Nate, Nathan.

12

HEATHER

You know that tingly little feeling
you get when you like someone?
That is your common sense leaving your body.

~ Unknown

Rene has been here again all day today. I'm not complaining. I should be. He's worn me down with his unexpected kindness, his flirting, and the way he listens when I talk. I never expected him to be so thoughtful or perceptive. I guess the latter trait goes with being a flirt—you have to learn to read the room, and every woman in it. But that's not really fair. While Rene is kind to every woman he sees, and many of them blush or swoon under his attention, he's never been inappropriate. If anything, he's reserved most of his laser focus for me. And it's making me crazy. I shouldn't be spending so much time thinking about a man who will be leaving to live over four thousand miles away.

Rene left for the afternoon. He's taking Nate out to ice cream.

Before they left, Nate said, "I'm gonna show you all the best spots in Harvest Hollow." As an afterthought, Nate looked at me and asked, "Can I, Mom?"

I said yes without a second thought. And now the two of them are out touring around while I'm covering the rest of the day here until closing. I had another interview this afternoon. A young woman named Adohi came in. She's an artist and needs to find what she calls a "day job" to support herself. I know most people don't plan to be a barista for life. Adohi seems reliable, so I hired her to start next week. I might even get a whole day off once she's trained.

The bell over the door tinkles and I look up to see my sister walking in.

"Hey, you!" I walk over to pull Tasha into a hug.

She's beaming with that special glow of mid-pregnancy hormones. She's actually been exuding this quiet radiance ever since she and Pierre decided to stay married. Love looks good on my sister.

"How are you holding up?" Tasha clasps my shoulders and holds me at arm's length so she can study my face.

"I hired someone today. She starts next week. The storm may be nearly over—this time."

"You look tired."

"Thanks?"

"And beautiful. But tired. I wish you would have told Melanie and Stan about the situation. But you're stubborn when it comes to accepting help."

"I am not! I even let Mom come in twice."

"As if you could have stopped her."

"Right?"

We walk toward the back counter on instinct.

"You should try this new blackberry-citrus tea I just got in."

"Um. Yes, please. That sounds amazing."

I step behind the counter and Tasha leans on the front while I brew her a cup, then we walk to a table along the wall.

"Sit with me. It feels like forever since we've talked." She slips into a chair and looks up at me.

"It's been forever since I've talked to any adult—besides Rene."

Why, oh why, did I bring him up to Tasha? She's going to be like a doberman with a steak.

Tasha takes a careful sip of her tea and wags her eyebrows. Her eyes bore into mine in a way only a sister's can. An interrogation room has nothing on her with its bare bulb and sparse furnishings. She's here to pull everything out of me, and she will get what she came for.

I spill like a stool pigeon looking at twenty to life.

"He's unnerving."

Tasha's grin says everything. It's nearly a smirk, but her eyes are soft and dreamy.

"And, by unnerving, you mean?"

I bury my face in my hands. "Gah!"

He's so handsome. "Agh!"

And he's kind. Why did he have to be so kind? "Ugh!"

And Nate adores him. "Ahhhhgh!"

When I look up, Tasha is beaming. "Yep. You've got it bad."

"No. I don't. I don't have anything—except a job that

takes all my spare time, and a child to raise, and the looming threat as to what I'm going to do when this place sells."

Tasha's forehead crinkles and her eyes go softer, if that's possible. "We won't let you fall, Heather. No way. No matter what. If something happens to Catty, we'll all make sure you land on your feet somehow. You might be a single mom, but you're not alone."

I nearly cry—and not merely from the impact of the truth of that safety net and the genuine care in my sister's expression and tone of voice, but everything. Just *everything*.

I eek out a soft, "Thanks." And then I look at my baby sister and smile. "You are going to make an amazing mom."

"I'm so scared. Pierre is going to be a great dad. He's so gentle and strong. You see him with Nate. He'll be as awesome as he is about everything else in life."

"And you will be fun and sweet and the softest place to land for this child. They come to us as babies for a reason. That way you can work your way up to them being seventeen and liking kissing."

"Oh, gosh! I can't even with Nate!"

We both laugh.

"But you're deflecting," Tasha says with a pointed look.

"From the subject of Rene?"

She points at me and pinches her lips to the side. "You know I'm not leaving until you pour out all your scrambled thoughts. Where is he anyway? I thought he was here today —like he is basically every waking moment."

"It's been so weird. He has been here a lot. And he won't let me pay him with anything more than a daily espresso and croissant."

"Hey. His vacation. If he wants to play barista, so be it."

"He's been such a surprise. It will be weird when he

leaves. But you know. He's like a fantasy. Not real. A guy like him ... he's the type to come in and sweep a woman off her feet and then go on to live his life without a second thought of what he left behind him."

"Okay. You tell yourself that."

Tasha sits sipping her tea. I don't say anything else. My head swirls with thoughts. Even saying what I did made it clear how I feel. If life were different, would I want Rene to be more to me? Probably. Even though Nate would have to adjust to a man in my life. Even though I'd have to make room in my already packed schedule to spend time with him. Even though I'd have to take a leap of faith to trust him. I think I would.

"Tasha, how do I know?"

"Know what?"

Her voice is soft and careful. She knows me well enough to know I'm fragile and rightfully wary when it comes to the subject of men or romance.

"How do I know when a man is worth taking the risk for? I can't just put myself out there. I have to consider Nate. And this man is from across the ocean." I search her face as if it holds the answers to all the confusion I've been suppressing the past week. "This is so insane!"

Tasha shakes her head lightly.

"Maybe I'd feel this way about every Frenchman I meet."

Tasha chuckles. "Do you think so? You didn't feel this way for Pierre. I'll be the first to tell you the whole French thing adds another layer of je ne se quois. But you and I both know it has nothing to do with any Frenchman. It's *this* Frenchman. And I understand your predicament. You're an amazing mom. And you always put Nate first. I'm not telling you to disregard your son, but I'm pretty sure he'd be tickled to see you and Rene pursue something. That boy is in love."

"True. They're out on an ice cream date and a tour of Harvest Hollow as we speak. But this is all silliness. Rene leaves in a week. Let's just forget I ever said anything. He's been fun. I'm glad I got to know him better. I had totally misjudged him the last few times we met."

"Mm hmm." Tasha puts her tea cup in the saucer and looks directly in my eyes. "If you recall, the man I married lived ... hmm ... oh, yes! Exactly where Rene lives. And we had so many more obstacles to overcome. Granted, I didn't have a child. But ..." She reaches across the table and places her hand over mine. "Don't shut the door to possibilities, okay?"

I nod just as the door to the shop flies open and my probably-over-sugared eight-year-old comes bounding through followed by the man who somehow makes a smile come to my face even when I'm tired and weary at the end of a long day. Rene scans the room and when he sees me, his smile is wide.

"I got a double scoop!" Nate says when he reaches our table. "And we went to Harvest Farms and all over!"

Rene walks up behind Nate, his steady presence a strong contrast to my son's unbridled rambunctiousness.

"I got the whole tour." Rene's eyes meet mine and he holds me in his gaze while something private and precious passes between us.

I look away. It's too tempting to indulge in his affection. That's what it is. I've been avoiding naming it, but after talking with Tasha, it's clear Rene's not just flirting for sport. I feel the tug between us. It's exhilarating—nearly intoxicating at times. And I can't afford to be under the influence.

It's Nate's night at my parents', so Tasha offers to take him when she goes. That leaves me, Rene and one table of high school girls working on Valentine's cards and eating our holiday-themed heart cookies and smoothies. It's nearly closing, so I flip the sign.

"You girls are welcome to stay while I clean up."

"Thanks, Miss Heather!" Stacey says with a bright smile. Her braces have white, pink, and red alternating bands. She, like everyone else, is head over heels for the upcoming holiday.

I smile at them and walk toward the back where Rene is dutifully washing dishes and singing a song in French. I lean against the wall near the door, watching him as he scrubs a dish, his exposed forearms flexing, his sleeves pushed up— for me. He's doing all this for me. The reality hits me like a punch. All these days, he's been faithfully coming here to silently support me. It's been for me.

He turns his head, water running down the dish in his hands.

He stops singing at the sight of me. A light flush stains his cheeks. The combination of that color and the end-of-the-day stubble on his face does things to me. Dormant places in my heart seem to shake loose. I have the surprising urge to stride across the room, take his cheeks in my hands and kiss him—really kiss him.

Instead, I grab the mop. It's a reliable second choice when faced with the option of kissing a hot Frenchman. I must be losing my ever-living marbles.

"That song sounded familiar," I say, because saying, *kiss me, now*, is not an option.

"It was *Pour Que Tu M'aimes Encore* by the French-Canadian, Celine Dion. It is a song of love." He lets those words hang in the air between us. "The singer is telling her beloved all the ways she will change or move heaven and earth to have their love again."

"Oh." And now the blush is up my face. I feel it, tingly and hot. "Time to mop!"

I raise the handle in my hand up into the air as if I'm hoisting a baton in the marching band, and then I grab the bucket and exit the kitchen like I'm being chased. Smooth, Heather. Really smooth.

The girls out front have made a red, white, and pink mess around their table, but they help me sweep and gather their clippings and the scattered glitter that will haunt me for months to come. Glitter. There should be laws against it —especially Valentine's glitter.

The girls leave, and Rene and I finish closing the shop. Then he walks me out into the cool evening air and we stand facing one another on the sidewalk. It's the kind of evening that makes things seem blurry and softer somehow, with the sky nearly dark and the street only partly filled with cars. Our town is simple, even though it's not as small as some others. People mostly work eight to five and then they head home to their families and eat around dining tables.

"What are your plans tonight, Cher? Your son is with your parents?"

Before I can think, I tell him my actual plans. "A long bath."

Rene and I are near enough that I can see the pattern of his irises. His breath comes in puffs of transparent white swirls into the air between us. He swallows hard and his Adam's apple bobs.

"Sorry. That was TMI, huh?"

"TMI?" His mouth quirks up into a crooked smile.

"Too much info ... information."

"Oh. No. No. It's fine." Rene's words come out in an uncharacteristic rush. "We take baths in France too. Of course. You know. To clean up, or relax." He shakes his head at himself. "Whatever the bath is for here, it's the same there. Anyway, a bath is good. You should relax."

He regains composure at the end. Of course he does. Rene is the most self-contained, self-assured man I've ever met, next to my brother-in-law who is far more reserved than Rene. I can't believe I thought Rene was shallow. There are layers to this man, and the vulnerable, off-kilter side is one I find endearing. I'm in so much trouble.

I should excuse myself to go take my bath ... only now I'll picture Rene's reaction when I step into the tub. But I can't help myself. I don't want to leave him just yet. All day we're moving around one another in the shop. The tasks and customers give us a safe barrier. Now, it's just the two of us with barely a ruler's length of space between us.

"What are you doing tonight?" I ask.

"Ah. Not a bath." He says it so sincerely that we both burst into laughter.

"Good to know."

Rene smiles down at me, the corners of his eyes still crinkled.

"Maybe a movie. Or ... I don't know. I have heard about trivia night at the place ... What is it called? Tequila Mockingbird?"

"Yes. That's the name. It's a take on the classic novel. Trivia night should be fun."

"Have you been?"

"Me? No. If I'm not here at the shop, I'm home with Nate, or at my folks' or my sister's."

Rene seems to consider something, and then he asks, "Do you want to join me? I promise to be horrible. You can perhaps save me from mortification. American trivia is not my strength. But if they ask about Harvest Hollow, I know a few things now, thanks to your son."

I study Rene's face, his strong jaw, the easy welcome of his eyes.

"Unless you need to take that bath," he adds with a wink.

Leave it to Rene to recover from any shred of embarrassment quickly enough to turn the tables.

My answer sounds like it comes from someone other than me. "Um. Yeah. Sure. I need to change, though."

"You really don't."

He reaches out and I almost pull back from the unexpected touch when he runs a hand down my hair. "You are beautiful."

I ignore his compliment and his soft caress. It should feel awkward—him touching me. But it feels so right.

"No. I really do. I'm a mess after running the shop all day."

"Okay. How about this? You go home. Change if you like. I'll pick you up. Is seven good?"

"Seven works."

"Good." He smiles down at me. "It's a date."

A date? A date, date? Or is that just a saying? Is he asking me out? Did I just say yes?

I feel like a pilot when the plane's instrument panel starts lighting up to say an engine failed ... and the wing fell off ... and we're being bombarded by a rogue flock of pigeons. All the bells and lights are sounding and blinking at once: *Mayday! Mayday!*

Rene leans in and kisses my cheek, just one cheek. It's such a brief brush of his lips to my face, I'm left wondering if it happened when he pulls away.

"Seven, then," he says.

I watch in stunned silence as he turns and walks to Pierre's car and leaves me standing in front of Cataloochee in a temporary paralysis.

I hop into my car and immediately call Hannah.

"Hey, Heather. What's up?"

"It's my night alone. I was going to take a bath. An innocent bath. Just me, in the bath. Alone."

"I should hope so." She giggles.

"Right. Anyway, Rene stayed late. Some girls from Harvest High were making Valentines. But they left and it was just the two of us."

"And he kissed you!"

"No! Stay with me here. This is an emergency!"

"Did he hurt you?"

"No! Of course not. He would never."

He *would* never. He would *never*. Oh my goodness. That makes everything so much worse. I finally met a man who would never, ever hurt me.

"Okay, so tell me what's going on. You sound like you did the time the espresso machine blew."

"It's worse. So much worse." I take a breath as I drive toward home. "He and I were outside the shop and I told him I was going to take a bath."

"What? Why?"

"Stop interrupting me! He asked. Okay?"

"He asked if you were going to take a bath?"

"No. Of course he didn't ask. He asked what I was doing and I said I was taking a bath. Alone."

"Oh, hunny. You really are rusty, aren't you?"

"Not helping. Not helping at all."

"Okay. Here's me. Zipping my lip. So, you give him the mental image of you in a tub and then what happened?"

"Agh! I did do that, didn't I?"

"Whatever. What happened next?"

"He asked me out."

There. I said it.

"Wait. You told him you were taking a bath, and he asked you out?"

"There were other things said, obviously ... between the bath and him asking me to Tequila Mockingbird ... but, yes. The upshot is he wants to take me to trivia night and he said, and I quote, 'It's a date.'"

"Woooo hoooo! Fine-ah-leeeee! I thought that man would never. I mean, yes, he's from across the ocean, but he's here. You're here. You need some romance. He can't keep his eyes off you. This is fabulous. Just fabulous."

"Are you *crazy*?"

"No. Are you? A hot, single, devoted, kind Frenchman wants to take you out on the town. You have built-in babysitting. What seems to be the problem?"

I sit with her question as I turn into my driveway. "Me. I'm the problem."

"There's a famous song about that."

"Ha. Ha."

"Seriously, Heath. You deserve a night out more than anyone else I know. Go. Get dressed. Wear something mid-level sexy. Nothing too bold, but something that says to him, *I heard you call this a date and I'm here for it.* You know?"

"No. I don't know. I know I need to get the crispy residue of cookie frosting out of one side of my hair and change out of this T-shirt I've been wearing since four a.m. But mid-level sexy is no longer in my wheelhouse. I don't think miniscule-level sexy is even in the repertoire."

"Girl. I wish you knew. You have that whole girl-next-door-but-more thing going for you."

"What?"

"Nevermind. I'm coming over. And I'm bringing tops. Take that bath, or a shower. I'll dress you. We won't go all red sweater dress level hotness this time, but he'll get an eyeful anyway. Ooo-wee. Someone's getting a kiss goodnight! I just know it."

"I'm not guaranteeing I'm up for that."

"Fine. No pressure. But it's a kiss. You are allowed to have a pastry here and there. Why not a very delicious kiss from a Frenchman?"

"For one thing, I'm sure he'd kiss me into next week. But I haven't kissed anyone in six years. I feel like my lips went into retirement. How will I know how to kiss him?"

"You'll know. Trust me. You'll know. Now hang up and go get ready so I can put my finishing touches on you."

I sigh. "I love you, Hannah."

"I love you, too."

13

HEATHER

Dating is different when you get older.
You're not as trusting, or as eager to
get back out there and expose yourself to someone.
~ Toni Braxton

H annah shows up after I step out of the bath and dry off. I'm in my best jeans and a robe when I answer the door.

"Okay, gorgeous. Let's get you date-ready."

"Let's not use that word. Okay?"

"Nope. No can do. Let's use that word until you believe it. Date, date, date. Rene is taking you on a date. You are date-able. Date-lectible. Date-tabulous. Date-a-licious. You're the date that's oh-so-great. Dater, dater, hot potater. This girl's going on a date!"

"All you lack are some pom-poms and your old cheer skirt."

"Which would fit over one leg these days!" Hannah laughs. "I was such a twig in high school."

"You might be a tad overzealous about what's going on between me and Rene. You know that, right?"

"I may be overcompensating just a wee bit for your complete under-zealousness. You've been that way for good reason, I get it. But six years is probably a long enough moratorium. So, tonight's the night you break that dry spell. And you've got just the man to help you see yourself as more than a mom and business manager. You have hit the European jackpot!"

I laugh. Then I throw my arms open. "Okay. Do your magic."

"That's the attitude."

We spend the next hour in my bedroom with me trying on blouses and v-neck sweaters until we land on a jewel-toned blouse that has sheer sleeves and a light V at the neckline that isn't too plunging. It wraps at the waist and has a bow that Hannah ties off to the side, just over my hip.

"Oh, girl. You look like a package he's going to want to unwrap."

"Stop. Please. You make my armpits breakout in a sweat when you talk like that."

"Sexy." Hannah laughs.

"Just dial it back. The pressure is already too much without all your extra insinuation that I'm going to be someone who matters or makes an impression."

Hannah pushes me onto a short stool I've placed in front of my bathroom mirror so she can do my makeup.

"Okay. Okay. But can I stay to see his reaction?"

"No. No way. That would be awkward. I just want to make this night no big deal."

"Okay. It's no big deal. Can I leave my phone here with the video camera rolling instead? I'll hide it somewhere discreet."

"Hannah!"

"Kidding! I just wish I could see his face when he first lays eyes on you."

"He sees me all day."

"With frosting in your hair and an outfit that looks like you're modeling for the children's Gap catalog. Not that you aren't beyond cute in all that too, but you clean up like a model, sweet friend."

"Right."

"Maybe it's better you don't know. You'd get all into yourself. Instead, half your appeal is how clueless you are as to your beauty and allure."

"You wear some extra-thick rose-colored glasses when it comes to me."

"Okay. Let's see if I'm right. Please, indulge me by telling me if he has any reaction whatsoever to you when you open the door. That's all I ask as restitution for my efforts here."

"Fine. I'll tell you."

Hannah finishes my makeup. Then she stands back and admires me with all sorts of unnecessary gushing. I try to quell my nerves while she packs up her bag of shirts, stashes her makeup, and gives me a quick and careful hug.

Her parting words are, "Details, Heather. I want details." And then she shuts the door and I hear her car pull away. About fifteen minutes later—fifteen minutes during which I attempted to read and then ended up tidying the front room instead—I hear a car in the driveway.

He's here.

My heart flutters to life with nerves and a zinging sensation I haven't felt in so long I barely recognize it.

Rene knocks firmly, three times. I walk to the door and open it.

He stands there, looking at me. And the look on his face makes me feel beautiful. He doesn't say anything, but he doesn't need to. His eyes take a slow tour of my face, warming with a soft crinkle at the edges as he glances at me. Then his gaze travels down as he takes in my outfit, and back up to meet my eyes. I hold on to the door edge, needing something for support. I should feel unnerved by his scrutiny, but instead, I feel emboldened and alive.

Rene looks like he put a little effort in too. His hair is almost always perfect, but tousled. He definitely did something to it since we parted outside Catty. He's clean shaven, and he smells like he put on cologne. It's a musky, masculine scent. When our eyes meet, I feel my heart rate escalate. He's definitely found the secret to whatever it is that makes me come to life. I'm a high-end sports car, and he's the professional driver with a set of keys and his foot on the pedal. I'm reckless and turbo-charged when his mouth tips up in a crooked grin.

"Ouah. Tu es si belle j'ai besoin d'un moment pour reprendre mon souffle."

I smile. "I don't know what you just said."

Something about a souffle?

"Breathtaking, Cher. You are breathtaking."

Oh.

He steps into my house, and now it's Rene and me, alone in my living room. His eyes rove around the walls and furniture. I follow the path he traces and see my home in a different light—modest, older, functional. I wonder what Rene's home in Avignon looks like.

"Here you have it." I wave my arm like a clumsy tour guide. "Home sweet home. It's simple, but good for the two of us."

"It is lovely." When he says that, his eyes are back on me with the same heat that used to feel contrived, but now sends a spark running through me.

"Shall we?" I need air.

"Of course. Do you have a coat?"

I grab my coat and Rene reaches for it, lifting it while I slip my arms into the sleeves, then he pulls the lapels around and pats them before stepping back and holding the door open. My mind inconveniently flashes to memories of Andrew taking me out on dates—even after we were married. He held my coat too. But Andrew wasn't Rene, and Rene definitely isn't Andrew.

"Did you eat?"

"Um. No, actually. I ..." I almost tell him I took the bath I had mentioned needing, but I stop myself before putting my foot in my mouth again. "I relaxed and got ready."

"Are you hungry?"

"A little."

We step out onto the porch and I lock the door. Then Rene places his palm on my back in the most unassuming way, leading me toward Pierre's car.

I'm actually really hungry, but I don't want Rene to feel like he has to get me food.

"Of course you are hungry. Let's see. You had a coffee while we were opening. But nothing to eat. Then you didn't eat until mid-day when you grabbed a banana and snuck into the kitchen to eat it quickly between customers. Unless you ate while I was out with Nate, you are living on a banana and coffee."

He holds open the passenger door and I stand there staring at him. I don't know if anyone has ever paid this much attention to such insignificant details about me and my life.

"Busted," I say softly.

"Let me feed you, Cher."

What does a woman say? Nothing, apparently. I merely look at him and have to stop myself from leaning in to either hug him or kiss him. I manage to break the pull Rene is having on me long enough to slip into the front seat and exhale a steadying breath while he rounds the car to take his place behind the wheel.

"Do they have food at this place we are going?"

"They do. Bar food mostly. But that actually sounds good."

"Okay. Bar food. C'est bon. Next time I will take you ... hmm ... to the place ... Ah! Yes. It's called Harvested."

"Harvested?"

Rene nods.

Next time? When does he think there will be a next time? He's leaving in a week.

"You have heard of this place, Harvested?"

"Of course. It's right down the street from Catty. It's a little fancy."

"Good. That is where we will go on our next date."

There it is ... that word.

"Our next date?"

"Oui. I am taking you out again. Maybe this weekend."

"Bossy."

It's all I can say. He is being bossy. He doesn't need to

know how much I actually like his take-charge approach right now. I make decisions all day. He also doesn't need to know what I'm feeling when he declares he'll be taking me out again. Cinderella had her pumpkins and mice. I have mine. But oh, that night of the ball! I'm going to give myself the chance to play princess just this once. Hannah's right. I need this.

Rene parks and we walk into Tequila Mockingbird looking very much like a couple. The hostess seats us at a high-top table. I hadn't thought this through. People I've known for years are trying to be subtle about the way they are staring at me and Rene. A few old friends from high school stop by to say, "Hi," or "It's good to see you out." Rene's natural charm settles my raging nerves. He's put his hand on my back several times as if we just go around touching one another all the time.

The trivia starts. Tonight's theme is ... of course ... Valentine's Day and Romantic Movies, Songs, and Books. Great. Surprisingly, Rene knows a lot of the history of the holiday. I know some of the romcom movies and songs, so we don't do too badly. But we don't win. I gorge on chicken wings and artichoke dip. We each sip a local IPA.

By the time we step into the chill night air, I'm smiling and relaxed.

"Let's walk," Rene suggests. "You have to get Nate, of course. But I'm not ready to end our night together yet. Do you have time?"

"Actually," I look up at him. "Nate is spending the night at my parents'. Dad will drive him to school in the morning for me."

"So you have no curfew?"

"Nope."

"Well then, let's enjoy a walk together. The street looks magical, non?"

"It does."

Rene reaches down and clasps my hand in his, then he shifts so our fingers are entwined. I don't know what it is about the lacing of fingers that feels so much more intimate than usual hand holding. We stroll in silence together down Maple Street toward the old library, and then to the town square where the fountain is backlit at night.

"That was nice," Rene says.

"It was. And we didn't completely stink at trivia."

"I haven't had that much fun in a long time."

"I find that hard to believe."

"Why?"

I glance over at him. Maybe it's the darkness, or the familiarity between us after working so closely together over the past week. I'm feeling bold.

"I picture you out with a different woman every weekend, dancing, drinking, romancing, breaking heart after heart."

Rene pauses and looks down at me. He turns so we are facing one another, but he doesn't drop my hand. His face is serious.

"I do go out. Oui. Dancing sometimes. I meet friends for drinks. I have dated. But I do not leave a trail of broken hearts. I have been ... maybe lonely? Maybe bored? Something has not been complete for me for some time now. And I didn't know my own mind until I came here. Your sister and Pierre talked me into this trip because I was pouting in my home one night. I miss my best friend. And I ... ach." He pauses for a minute, looking into the distance over my shoulder. When he looks back at me, his face holds a vulnerability I've never seen in him before. "I always thought it would be enough: success in business, a good social life, my family. But lately, it feels a little empty."

Rene cups my cheek. His hand is warm. I tilt just the slightest to keep him from pulling it away.

"When I came to America, I was so lost that I didn't even know I was lost. That is si tragique."

Tragic. I get that one.

"In your shop, I have been able to find something."

His hand is still on my cheek and I'm fighting one recurring thought: *Will he kiss me now?*

Rene's pouring out his heart and I'm thinking about how his lips would feel on mine. I refocus on his words.

"I'm so glad you've been able to find something at Cataloochee. It's part of what I hope to cultivate—maybe a haven? A gathering place. I want people to be able to pause or pull back from life, and also to take time to connect with one another. We're all so busy, at least in the states we are. People need a place to remind them to stop and slow down, to savor, reflect, and connect. Cataloochee can be that place."

Rene's smile is full.

"Oui. It is obvious. You make everyone feel so welcome—like they belong there."

I smile back at him. He drops his hand and I miss the contact, especially when he turns and starts leading us around the town square again.

"Thank you for sharing all of that with me. I am sorry I assumed so much about you. I know you better now. I ..."

He smirks over at me, never one to shy away from receiving a compliment.

I look up at him, knowing nothing can come of this confession, but still needing him to know. "I like you a lot."

"Mmm. I like you a lot too, Cher. Very much."

We walk quietly again, and it's more comfortable than I would have expected. Rene can be a little like Nate: playful, exuberant, a loud presence. But he's a man—all man. And when the time to get serious comes, he has everything it takes to shift gears and show a far more mature side to himself. My mind entertains itself thinking about all the sides of Rene as we walk, hand-in-hand, through the only town I've ever called home.

After we walk back to the car, Rene drives me back to my house. He grabs my hand once we're buckled and holds it the whole ride, brushing softly across the top of my thumb with his. I don't resist him, and I don't question him either. I'm wearing my glass slippers. Midnight will strike soon enough.

When he unbuckles and steps out of the car, my brain snaps into panic mode. Our date is over. The moment of reckoning has arrived.

Do I want him to kiss me or not?

Rene goes through the motions of opening the car door for me, leading me to my porch, and then we stand, facing one another. I could ask him inside for something warm to drink, but I don't trust myself to even make the suggestion.

"I had a very nice night with you. Did you enjoy our date, mon ange?"

I've heard Pierre use that term of endearment with my sister. It feels different coming from Rene to me.

"I did. It ..." *Should I tell him?*

I blurt out the fact quickly, looking away to avoid seeing Rene's reaction. "It was the first date since my divorce."

The air is still and quiet as if my profession stopped time. Then Rene carefully reaches up and cups my face in his hands. He gently turns my head so I'm looking directly into his bright green eyes.

"I am honored that you would go out with me. I did not know you had not been out with a man since your divorce. But it makes sense. You are a busy woman—a mother. But also, it does not make any sense that you would not be dating. Even today, that man, Brennan, came to the shop very much intending to ask you out. You must have known that."

"I did. I just ... I haven't seen him much since high school. I'm not really looking to start dating." I nearly kick myself for saying those words to Rene. I want to quickly tack on, *Unless it's you.* But that's an exercise in futility. We both know this time between us is dwindling and we'll be on separate continents by this time next week.

"Cher, you are in your head all the time." Rene taps my temple lightly, and it might possibly be the most intimate way a man has ever touched me.

"Come down out of there for just a little while. Relax. You can just be here, no? Just enjoy a man taking you out and calling you beautiful. Enjoy making me feel things I haven't felt in years—maybe ever. Give your brain a rest."

He taps my temple lightly again. "Stop living here." And then he moves his hand to the spot over my heart. "Use this instead, just for tonight."

And I want to. So badly. Rene has no idea. If I take his advice, following him blindly like Hansel and Gretel down a sexy, alluring path that leads to all my feelings for this unexpected man—this kind, sweet, funny, flirty, surprisingly compassionate man—there will be no coming back.

No. Staying in my brain is safe—far, far from emotions that will bake me alive if I give in to them.

I'm aware of this tiny squeak of frustration that comes out of my mouth. It's the same noise my mom used to make when I was a teen and I had pushed her too far. Funny how we grow up to take on so many of the same mannerisms we disparaged in our own parents.

Rene's eyes are soft when I look up at him. "Talk to me, Cher."

Talking. Here we are on my porch at the end of a wonderful night and we're talking because I can't get a grip on myself. I could have had a kiss. Instead, I'm getting therapy from my brother-in-law's best friend. Stellar.

"It's all ... fine. I guess. I just don't think so clearly with you around."

"Are you saying I'm a distraction?" Rene wags his eyebrows.

We're no longer holding hands and his palm has left my face, but I feel Rene's nearness as if he were holding me.

I laugh at his playfulness, and can't wipe the smile off my face at the realization of how easy it is for him to lighten the mood right at the moment I'm starting to plummet.

I barely register Rene's movements as he steps closer to me. His hand reaches out and brushes down my arm.

What were we even talking about?

When his hand meets mine, he gently flips my palm up and bends so his lips meet my hand. Then he's kissing along the pad of my thumb, grazing his lips over the sensitive skin between my fingers and my wrist. No one has ever kissed my hand. Or if they have, they definitely didn't do it right. Rene —well, he's doing it right. So right. I feel wobbly. Which only goes to show how long it's been since any man has kissed me anywhere.

My breath hitches. I have no game. Unless you count Mario Brothers matches with Nate.

No. game.

I'm an open book—obviously wanting Rene, and unable to hide the effect he has on me.

I reluctantly, but firmly extract my hand from Rene's grasp and rest it on my thigh like it's a child sent to time out. Bad, bad hand. No more of that for you. If hands could pout, mine is definitely throwing a tantrum.

Rene lifts his head and smiles calmly at me. He's not put out by my blatant reaction to his kisses. If anything, he's amused, but not in a way that mocks me. He's being patient, and his patience makes me all the more impatient—with myself, with our circumstances. It's not fair. After all these years, I open up. And my heart picks the most unattainable man possible.

"I'm kind of a hot mess," I explain. "Well, not kind of. I'm a complete and utter disaster. Maybe not at work. I know what I'm doing at the shop, and I do it well. But in here," I pat my heart and then tap my pointer to my temple. "In here, I'm a big mess. Certifiable. Confused. Just ..."

"Not true," Rene says quickly and with such conviction I'm almost convinced he's right. "You know I want you. You see how I am drawn to you. I might be flirtatious, but I do not flirt with every beautiful woman.

"It's you." Rene cups my cheek again. "Either you want me, too, or you don't. It's actually very simple."

He reaches for my hand again and runs a single finger up from my palm, over my wrist and then up my forearm. My coat mutes some of his touch, but not enough. I feel a chill run through me as if he were tracing a line up my bare skin. Rene continues to leave a trail of goosebumps up my upper arm and then my neck, and when his hand cups the back of my head to draw me in, I don't stand my ground.

"Simple," he whispers.

"Simple," I echo, almost mindlessly. I even feel myself nodding. At what, I'm not sure. Rene brushes his fingertips along the back of my neck and I shiver. He chuckles, obviously delighted in the powerful impact he's having over me.

Before my brain can engage or my words become cohesive, his lips are on mine. First, softly, tentatively, just the faintest brush across my mouth.

I lean in, dazed—grateful for the way his hand is still cupping my head. Maybe it would just loll over and my neck would stop supporting it. I feel like jello, but jello that could be used as a conduit for an electrical current. I'm a buzzing, warm, jiggly mess of a woman. Rene apparently isn't finished rocking my world. His other hand loops behind my waist and he tugs me toward himself. He stares into my eyes with this look of intensity and wonder that threatens to undo me.

"Beautiful," he whispers.

I almost ask, *me?*, but he's said it frequently enough with that sincere look in his eyes that I nearly believe him.

He makes me feel gorgeous, even sexy. I don't know the last time I felt sexy.

"Vous êtes la plus belle femme."

There he goes with the French words. And he's barely speaking, he's breathing the words across my cheek, into my ear, like they are a secret only we share. He could be saying there's a cobweb on the ceiling at the back corner of my porch. I've seen some. I just don't have the time or energy to get out here to knock them down. I have to get a ladder out and swipe at them. And this is what I'm thinking right now while Rene's warm breath travels from my ear, past my cheek?

I honestly don't care what he's saying. I still can't make out the murmured phrases. It's lovely and hypnotic and I just want him to keep saying anything in French.

But the part of me that needs to know things needs to know.

"Translate, please?"

"Oh, Cher. I said you are the most beautiful woman I've ever seen."

"What?" I pull back slightly. My inability to take a compliment nearly ruins the moment like a glass of ice water to the face.

"Cher," he coos. "Come here." His hand, now on my hip, gives a tug to emphasize where *here* is. Oh. There. Right there. Nestled in his arms.

"Okay," I breathe out in a far too breathy voice. It's not sexy, trust me. It's more of a gasp that might indicate I should see a pulmonologist.

Rene smooths my hair and then he looks at me again. "You are beautiful. And strong. And lovely. Funny." He pauses. His eyes rove around my face, cataloging my features. "Captivating."

I let out a short huff of laughter.

"You don't believe me? Ask me what my first thought has been each morning this week? And when I am alone in my bedroom at night? What are my thoughts drifting to?"

He's so blunt. No shame. No pretense.

I don't ask him. I know. I don't know why. But I know. Maybe I'm a novelty to him, something that is fascinating because it's new and different.

Before I can debate with him or negate his impression,

Rene leans in and kisses that sensitive spot between my neck and my shoulder—a spot that hasn't been touched in years unless you count my loofa and my son blowing the occasional raspberry there. This is no raspberry, but Rene's mouth has left me tingling and giddy all the same.

Then he leans in and kisses a sweet, soft trail of feather light kisses down my cheekbone, on the tip of my nose, and then at the corner of my mouth. I turn toward him, wrapping my arms around his neck and pulling him in. My mind shuts down—finally—and I am here with him as if all the world has been wiped away like a calculus formula on a whiteboard and all that remains is the silhouette of two people kissing on a porch in the moonlight.

His grasp of me is strong and secure, and my hands have taken on a life of their own, roaming through his wavy hair, toying with the nape of his neck, one cupping his face, feeling the smoothness of his skin and the edge of his jaw on my palm. The same palm he kissed only moments ago. Or was it days, or years? Time is nothing. Only us. Only this kiss which is now deepening and consuming me. I hear soft noises, little hums of appreciation, first in a quiet soprano. Those are my noises. He's making me hum. And then I hear the echoing rumble of Rene's satisfaction from deep in his throat. I feel like I weigh nothing. I'm light and bliss and freedom.

Slowly, my brain comes back on board. Nate. The shop. My life. My responsibilities. The ocean between us. Rene's life in France.

I step back, running a hand through my hair, barely able to look Rene in the eyes.

14

RENE

*Everyone knows that dating in your thirties
is not the happy-go-lucky free-for-all
it was when you were twenty-two.*

~ Helen Fielding, Bridget Jones's Diary

Heather's gone again—up into her thoughts. The worry is etched across her face as if she's been unfaithful to a vow. I'm still holding her, not willing to let go until she settles. She's likely to dart off like a skittish alley cat, and then she'll end up avoiding me for the last week we have together. For a few minutes, she was mine, here with me, responding to every touch, matching my kisses with her own.

I run my hand down her hair and tuck her head under my chin.

"Cher." I make a shushing sound, much like the one my mother used to calm me when I was a boy. "Heather."

She softens in my arms.

"Sorry."

"For kissing me, or for stopping?"

She wraps her arms behind me. A good sign. "Both?"

"No. That kiss—it was a gift. Please do not regret it, or me."

"I don't." Her head leans in, nestling deeper into my coat. I run my hands down her hair. "It's just so out of character for me. And I have Nate, and the shop. And you are in France and I'm here and this wasn't … you probably don't … I should shut up now."

Heather tilts her head up to look at me. I smile down at her. She returns my smile. It's a soft smile, full of trust, but tinged with sadness and questions.

"We do live on separate continents. And I know you have many responsibilities. We both knew that when we went out tonight. And tonight was everything, maybe it was even inevitable. We have been dancing around one another all week. It was bound to happen. Non? Even though we can't be more to one another than what we are.

"Please. Do not make this night less than it was—for either of us. You did not imagine the way I held you, or the urge I felt to always have my hand on your back, or your hand in mine. The connection between us isn't something simple or meaningless. You matter to me, Cher. I would not play with your heart. I absolutely would not kiss you if I thought it would send you into a whirlwind of regret."

"Okay."

"It would be nice if you fell in love with France and decided to open a cafe there," I joke.

"Sure. I'll just do that. Nate will be fine relocating, right?"

"We do have ice cream there."

"Sold."

We both laugh, but it is a hollow laughter filled with the awareness of our reality.

"I had a wonderful night with you, Heather. It is a night I will think back on when I'm in Avignon. If I am lonely, I will remember holding you here, and this memory will make me smile. And I am still taking you to Harvested."

"Okay."

"Okay?" I tilt back to see her face.

"Yes. You can take me to Harvested."

"And you can wear your red dress."

"Oh, I can, can I?"

"Oui. That dress ..."

"Is Hannah's."

"Hannah's?"

"I borrowed it."

"Why?"

Even in the darkness, I know she is blushing. I brush my hand across her cheek. "You wore it for me?"

"Maybe."

"Oh, Cher."

She dressed up for me. Even before I had convinced myself to ask her out. A week ago, she was dressing like that for me.

"I had better get some sleep," she says. "The morning alarm comes too soon."

"Thank you," I kiss her temple and draw her into another hug.

"For what?"

"For allowing me to be the one who took you on a date. I am honored."

"Thank you for taking me out. You reminded me I'm more than a mom and a woman running a business."

"You are so much more."

Heather smiles and then she goes up on her tiptoes and kisses my cheek. I turn my face and capture her mouth in a kiss. She kisses me back, looping her hand behind my neck. I pull her in, making this kiss matter, leaving her a souvenir, pouring my heart into this moment between us.

When she pulls away, she is smiling up at me.

"Goodnight, Rene."

"Goodnight, mon ange. Sweet dreams."

I step backward and Heather lets herself into her home. She turns and smiles at me before shutting the door. I walk back to Pierre's car, wondering why life sometimes leads us down paths lined with everything we ever dreamed we could have, only to show us they are a dead end.

But I push those thoughts aside. I'll have a lifetime to miss Heather, to think of her living here in Harvest Hollow while I carry on with my life in France. This week I will give myself the gift of enjoying her. I smile thinking of our kisses —the best kisses of my life because my heart was as engaged as my body. She tells me I am dangerous, but I think I may be the one in danger.

Pierre is sitting on the sofa in the living room when I walk in the door of his house fifteen minutes after saying goodnight to Heather. A lamp on the side table spreads a warm yellow glow through the room. The fire has burnt to embers in the fireplace. Tasha seems to have gone to bed, since there is no sign of her.

"Nice night?" Pierre asks after I shut the door behind me.

"Yes. Very nice. You?"

"Oui. Tasha cooked soup and bread. Then we sat here, reading together. But she gets tired early with the pregnancy, so she went up without me. I decided to wait up for you."

"To scold me?"

He smiles at me. I sit in the upholstered armchair across from him.

"Not to scold you. Do you need a scolding?"

"No."

We are quiet for a while after this, comfortable in the familiarity of our friendship.

Finally, he speaks. "So, you took Heather to trivia night?"

"Oui."

Pierre steeples his fingers under his chin.

I hold his gaze. I did nothing wrong tonight. I invited Heather out for an evening. She agreed. She even dressed up and put makeup on—a sign she agreed our evening was a date. And the way she kissed me ...

"What is that look?" Pierre asks.

"What look?"

"You look ... dreamy."

"I look dreamy?"

"Like you are imagining your mother's Bûche de Noel."

I laugh. I am not imagining the once-a-year dessert my maman makes for Christmas.

"No. Something delicious, but not a sweet."

"Rene." Pierre's tone borders on chiding.

"Pierre."

"Did you kiss Heather?"

"Maybe we kissed one another. Am I supposed to tell you? That would be a terrible way to treat a woman—to kiss her, and then to turn around and speak about it with someone else. Do you not agree?"

"I think I recall you pressing me for details about Tasha."

"Only to goad you into action. You were so blind."

"Well, no one needs to goad you into action. Do they?"

"Rarely. In this case, I had a delightful night. Heather also had a night that left her smiling. I will leave it at that."

My face falls slightly when I think of the reality. I will leave in a week. This isn't casual, at least to my heart it isn't. I started out wanting to help Heather relax and see herself as a woman who could have everything other women have—especially a man who cherishes her. But now, I am tangled inside. I no longer want her to find another man, and yet I cannot be the man who takes her out, gets to know her, and perhaps, eventually, makes a future with her and Nate.

"Now what?" Pierre asks.

"I have a problem."

Pierre sits patiently waiting for me to expound.

"I came to America and I met an incredible woman—she is beautiful, smart, driven, sexy, and she challenges me. But now I have to return to France without her. Our situation is impossible." I sigh. "Please, do not say you told me to be cautious. I am already suffering without the added weight of your admonishment."

"I don't know what to say. When I warned you away from Heather, it was because I know you enjoy flirting. I always have her history in mind, and I wanted to protect her—to let you know not to take anything with her as lightly as you might with another woman."

I nod. He is not wrong, even though I have been far more solitary than he thinks over the past year or so.

"And she has a son," I lament. "What do I know about being a father? Not that I'm in the position to be Nate's father. I'm not, obviously. I am going back to Avignon. I don't need to worry about being a father to an eight-year-old."

Pierre ignores my dismissal. "What do any of us know about being a parent? You love Nate. That much is obvious. You may not want to say you love Heather yet, and that makes sense. But you love that boy, and he loves you. I don't think you could have a better start than that if the situation ever turned into something more serious."

As much as Pierre's words bring me a sliver of hope, I can't afford to indulge in the picture he is painting—one where Heather and Nate and I become a family.

"I've only just gotten to know Heather these past two weeks, even though we really met when you started dating Tasha. It is too soon to feel so much for her. Do you not agree?"

"We are not teenagers. We are old enough to know what we want in life—and in our relationships. You have dated plenty of women, and none of them ever made you reconsider the trajectory of your life. None of them made you have talks like this with me. That says something. Only you can decide what it means and what you do once you figure yourself out."

Pierre smiles a playful smile and adds, "I have this friend. I think he would tell you to open your eyes and choose well."

"Wise, wise, friend." I chuckle.

"I never imagined you would fall for my sister-in-law." Pierre shakes his head.

Him and I both. I never imagined I'd fall for anyone, least of all an American.

"I don't know if I have fallen. It is still too new. But I am caught. That is certain. I have never felt like this before."

"Trust me, worse things have happened to a man. Even ..." Pierre winks at me. "... to a Frenchman."

15

HEATHER

Real love is as practical as it is magical.
~ Ruby Dhal

"Mom, why are you singing?"

Nate has his hands dramatically placed over his ears. My mom dropped him off here this morning since it's not a school day. Tasha's picking him up later. I woke feeling more blissed out than I have in years. And then the panic set in. *What have I done?* I lay there with the proverbial devil and angel on my shoulders, only I couldn't tell which was which.

One voice was reveling in Rene's touches, his kind words, the way he held me—I felt like he was holding me together and somehow setting me free at the same time. And then our kisses. I thought my lips wouldn't know what to do. But they deserve a merit badge for their performance.

The other voice kept reminding me of his real address, which I conveniently don't even know. But it's in *France*. And Nate. I thought of Nate. Sure, he loves Rene, but he would probably flip out at the idea of me dating or kissing anyone. Not that it's especially his business. But I can't help factoring my son into every decision I make. That's been my default for eight years. Nate matters. My choices affect him. And what if Rene and I messed up the equilibrium of our family dynamic with Pierre and Tasha by going on a date and letting all our captive feelings for one another out into the wild?

My mind spun and my heart raced on alternating tracks. One made me feel like a teenager again. The other reminded me how very-much-not-a-teen I truly am.

At least I was alone this morning. I had a full forty-five minutes to overthink the date with Rene over coffee, in the shower, while I dressed, on my short commute to the shop.

And then I saw him, standing outside the door, waiting for me with a smile that made me feel all gooey and light-headed. When I stepped out of my car I had a moment of wondering what would happen. Would it be awkward? How should I act? Man, my overthinking skills had failed me. I had completely forgotten to stress over the first time I would see Rene with his perfectly tousled wavy hair and his gentle, but playful eyes, and a scruff on his jaw that told me he hadn't shaved since cleaning himself up for our date. I wanted to reach out and run my hand along his jaw—right there in the inky light of pre-dawn morning on Maple.

I should have known Rene would handle everything, including my nerves. He beamed a smile at me that was tinged with longing. But that smile managed to smooth out all my jagged thoughts in an instant.

Then he spoke. "Bonjour, mon ange. You slept well?"

He stepped near to me and wrapped an arm around my shoulder and softly placed his lips to my temple. It was the sweetest gesture, not a trace of playfulness or desire was involved. I felt like I was his to hold, his to kiss, his to comfort and support. It's a heady experience when a man like Rene harnesses all that charisma and care, and chooses me as the sole recipient. I'm still floating around the shop— from a simple French greeting and a kiss to my temple.

I had tilted my head, cupped his jaw and kissed the side of his cheek, allowing my lips to linger there long enough to breathe him in and feel the warmth between us. Then I moved away from his embrace and unlocked the door. We were both quiet, not needing words. That, too, is new. He had unnerved me for the past few years. Initially, he just made me wary and set off my inner critic. Then he put me on my ear. I didn't know how to reconcile his thoughtfulness with the ease he seemed to have around women. And now, I feel more at home with him than I have with anyone outside my family. It's strange, but I'm in no mood to analyze this. We both know there are exactly six days until he leaves. And that fact is one I want to ignore fully.

What will happen? my unhelpful brain taunts.

I don't care, I tell myself.

I will ride this sweet experience like the roller coaster it is, and then disembark, leave the magic and whimsy of the theme park and go back to my straightforward, uneventful life without Rene. Simple. Not easy.

"I'm singing because I'm happy," I tell Nate.

"Don't. You sound weird."

"Oh, really? Is that a kind way to speak to someone, especially your own mother?"

"Believe me, Mom. It's kind. If you could hear yourself, you'd know I'm doing you a favor."

My son. Sheesh.

"How about humming?" I tease.

"I'll let you know."

I start humming and move through the kitchen into the pantry to grab what I came back here for.

The day is busy—as Saturdays are. Simon does a great job filling in, and for the first time since Cedar gave his resignation, I feel like I'll be able to manage again without losing my mind.

Just after the lunch rush, a package arrives at the back door. I'm not expecting a delivery. The courier hands me a box and asks me to sign. I can barely manage to scribble my name with the stylus while propping the wide, flat, white cardboard box carefully between my hip and the door jamb.

I shut the door behind the delivery guy and stare at the package in my arms. The cardboard is the consistency of a gift box, not thick like you'd use for shipping. A red satin bow is elegantly looped around the middle. My life consists of picking up max-packs of granny undies and a few nondescript T-shirts at Walmart when my supply wears thin. This package feels so foreign and decadent in my arms.

Rene has slipped out for the past two hours, saying he had errands to run just as Tasha arrived to pick up Nate. And now, I am beyond curious as to what his errands actually entailed.

I'm alone in the kitchen, so I set the box on the metal island at the center of the room. I carefully lift the card out from the spot where it's tucked neatly under the ribbon. I shouldn't be surprised, but a small gasp falls from my mouth when I read "For Heather, mon ange" in a beautifully penned font on the front of the envelope.

His angel. I asked Google to translate that phrase this morning while I sat, sipping a five-minute cup of coffee in the quiet of my living room. I'm no angel, and I'm not his, but for this week ... I'm pretending.

I slip the note out, feeling like a kid at Christmas, but one who never had a tree or stocking. *Magical.* He makes me feel like the world is full of possibilities, and I'm his greatest one. I quickly shut down the counter-thought that follows my dreaminess. For the first time ever, I'm riding the romance train. I refuse to let my practical side rob me of one drop of this once-in-a-lifetime experience.

I slowly read the note, taking in every word. While the name on the envelope was written by someone else, this is a man's penmanship: Rene's.

Mon ange, Heather,

I know you are vehemently opposed to Valentine's Day. And I have been in agreement with you until last night. I won't try to change your mind. Just go with me to Harvested on Maple in this dress before I have to leave for my trip home. I promise to behave like a gentleman even though the sight of you makes me want to behave in ways I won't put in a card because Nate might find this.

(Hi Nate. If you are reading this, stop. I have grown-up things to say to your mom).

I giggle in the solitude of the kitchen, and reach up to swipe a tear trailing down my cheek.

I've asked your parents to host a certain eight-year-old for an overnight. Simon agreed to close up Cataloochee for us.

Us! If only there could be an us.

Tomorrow night, on Valentine's Day, you can leave early. Simon and I will cover the afternoon so you can take your time being pampered and getting ready. Hannah has all the details for you about that part of our evening together. Then, you will text me when you want me to swing by to pick you up. I'll be the guy in a gray suit, standing on your porch—the one who can't keep his eyes off you. J'ai hâte de vous gâter comme vous le méritez.

Je suis à toi (I am yours)
- Rene

I read the card again, and then, as if I'm the heroine in some romance movie, I clutch the paper to my chest and sigh. *Rene.*

I look at the box. A dress is in there. Obviously. It can wait one more minute while I translate that one last sentence in Rene's note. I stare at the translator on my phone when the sentence pops up: *I can't wait to spoil you like you deserve.* How does he see me? And how did he ever get me to start seeing myself through the same lens as the one he uses? *Magic.* He is magic. Maybe he's not even real. I'm starting to wonder. Here I am, the most practical person I know, and I'm giddy over a dress in a box and the man who sent it.

I carefully tug at the satin ribbon on the box and it slides across itself, falling into twin pools of red on either side of the package. Then I cautiously lift the lid. Inside, the dress is wrapped in a fancy tissue paper, with one gold sticker sealing the seam. I gingerly tug the sticker, hoping to preserve every single thing about this moment. I'll only have these mementos of paper and fabric once February passes me by.

The dress is red. Of course it is. I pull it out and hold it up to myself. I have no doubt it will fit. Isn't this how fantasies work? Everything fits. The details fall into place. The couple waltzes into their happily ever after with twin dreamy looks in their eyes. For six more days, I'll permit myself to believe in real-life fairy tales. When I'm old and alone, I'll look back on this week and thank my younger self for letting go and allowing myself to enjoy a man like Rene without hesitation or second-guesses.

I fold the dress, taking care to tuck it back into the box like a rare artifact. Considering I'll only wear it once, it practically is one.

I text Rene.

Heather: *You're too much.*
Rene: *You are very right. I am.*
Heather: *Thank you.*
Rene: *For you, anything.*

I smile softly to myself. My hand rests over my racing heart.

Then I call Hannah.

16

RENE

He calls me beautiful, like it's my name.

~ Unknown

I'm dressed in a suit I packed with me because, well, I'm French. Not that we strut around in suits, but in our cities, we tend to dress more formally than most Americans. For tonight, I want to look so good that Heather can't take her eyes off me. Since I won't be able to stop staring at her, it is only fair to return the favor.

She called me right after she left Catty Coffee, a lightness in her voice that I've never heard before. What is it about affection that changes the voice and the eyes? When we look at one another I feel as if someone is humming my favorite song. Just the sound of her voice over the phone made me spark to life with a nearly electric feeling, and I had only seen her twenty minutes before the call.

I was still in the shop with Simon, even though there

were very few customers left at the tables. I stepped into the kitchen to take Heather's call, out of earshot from patrons or Simon.

"Rene! You got us mani/pedis?"

"Oui. Do you like those?"

"I love them. Do you know how long it has been since I got my nails done?"

"No."

"So long. Maybe before Nate was born. This is ... decadent."

"You are worth it."

She was silent long enough for me to sense everything she was not saying. I smiled the whole time. She may think she is being spoiled, but I am the one experiencing something I have never had before—the opportunity to pamper a woman who means so much to me. Nothing has ever made me so happy.

After we hung up, I stayed at the shop with Simon. An hour later, I left, coming back to Pierre's to get ready for a night I am quite sure I will never forget. I shaved, put on cologne, ironed my shirt, steamed my pants, and then I dressed. Finally, I finished my hair, and here I sit, waiting for Heather's text. Pierre has been teasing me and Tasha keeps gushing over the fact that I am taking her sister out for Valentine's. The two of them are having a private candlelight dinner at home, just Pierre's style.

Finally, Heather texts me.

Heather: *I am ready.*

Rene: *Give me ten minutes and I will be at your door.*

I quickly grab my coat and put it on.

"Are you off?" Pierre asks from the kitchen where he is preparing the food for his dinner with Tasha.

"I am. Don't wait up."

He chuckles. "Have a great night."

"How can I not?"

My phone buzzes with Heather's next text as I step out the door.

> **Heather:** *I'm excited and nervous. Just to be honest.*
> **Rene:** *Me too. I am also excited and nervous. You make me very nervous.*
> **Heather:** *Are you just saying that to make me feel better?*
> **Rene:** *You would feel better if I were suffering with nerves?*
> **Heather:** *I wouldn't feel so alone in my nerves.*

I turn the car key and send my last text before I pull away from Pierre and Tasha's home.

> **Rene:** *I have never felt this way. You make me feel so many things. And that makes me nervous because I want to do everything right. I don't want to disappoint you.*

I glance down to read Heather's response.

> **Heather:** *You could never.*

Smiling, I pocket my phone and drive to Heather's, going only a little over the speed limit. My eager foot keeps pressing the gas pedal too hard. I can't get to Heather quickly enough. Now that we have openly admitted our feelings for one another, I find it difficult to be away from her. She is on my mind constantly, and I miss her, even though I am still in her hometown.

I park in Heather's driveway and force myself to walk from the car to the front door as if I'm not clawing away inside myself to see her in that dress. I have Hannah to thank for so many details of this evening. She met me at a boutique in town to pick the dress, providing Heather's size and consulting on the choices until we found just the right one. And then she helped me arrange the afternoon of pampering that Heather enjoyed today. I made the reservations at Harvested—a table for two near the window.

I knock on the door, putting my hands in my pockets and then removing them quickly, trying different ways of standing so I look casual and composed. I am quite sure not one of them is convincing. Heather's heels click across her wood floors and then the door opens and she is standing there, wearing the red dress with black heels. Her hair has waves curled into it, and her lipstick matches the dress.

"Well, hello," Heather says. Her eyes roam from the top of my head to my polished shoes and back up to my face. "Wow. You look very handsome." She blushes a little and then says, "Let me get my coat."

"You look more beautiful than I imagined you would. And that is saying something, because I have a very vivid imagination."

"Aww. This old thing?" She turns and winks at me.

I step inside, taking her coat from her. The dress has what the saleswoman called capped sleeves. They flutter off Heather's shoulders and leave her arms exposed. I slip the coat on from behind her, allowing my fingers to graze her skin as I do.

Heather turns around and surprises me by cupping my face in her hands.

"You didn't give me cheek kisses," she chides me.

"I thought you wanted me to stop those," I tease.

Heather shakes her head lightly and then she kisses each of my cheeks gently. I am so overwhelmed by her boldness, the smell of her perfume, and the way she looks, it is only after she pulls back that I realize I didn't kiss her in return.

She swipes at one of my cheeks with her thumb. "You had a little lipstick there."

"I want to kiss you now, Cher. But we have a reservation, and maybe it is better I wait until after dinner, or I may never let you leave this house."

She giggles. "Rene. You say things I never thought a man would say to me. You make me feel ... like I'm all you want."

"Because you are, Cher. Now, let's go celebrate this saint who secretly married lovers when his government outlawed marriage."

"Is that what we are celebrating?" Heather laughs.

"No, Cher. I am celebrating you. Only you."

We drive to Harvested, Heather's hand in mine. I can't help glancing over at her while we drive. We find parking a block away from the restaurant. Tonight, Harvest Hollow is buzzing with people, the sidewalks are filled with couples holding hands and gazing into one another's eyes. We are not one of many, though. I know in my heart what we have is special, even if we face an end date. Maybe what we have is all the more special because we know we can not keep it. We aren't under the illusion that this will be one more Valentine's Day in a string of shared holidays. This is it: our one Valentine's Day together. I cut my thoughts off before they travel into morbidity.

Heather squeezes my hand. "Thank you for this day. It felt amazing to be so pampered. Hannah kept joking, telling me if I didn't want you, she'd gladly take you off my hands."

"Mmm. Hannah is a good friend. I'm not interested in her offer, though. Not at all. The only woman I want is here with me now."

"Good. You know, in high school, she was the head cheerleader. All the boys wanted to date her. I was a bit more bookish and interested in things like hiking and kayaking. We were the best of friends, so I never felt too jealous of all the attention she got from the guys at school."

"She's not you."

Heather looks up at me. Her eyes are soft and misty. "No one ever felt that way about me. Even Andrew paid special attention to Hannah when he first came to visit me from Asheville in our early years of dating. Hannah brushed Andrew off. She had a boyfriend at the time. And I didn't see it—how easily he could set me aside for someone else. I just chalked it up to Hannah being so much more beautiful and engaging ... more everything."

"Andrew was a fool. I could never set you aside for someone else." It's the first time I've spoken his name and I despise the sound of it coming from my mouth.

"I'm sorry. I don't know why I'm talking about him. Here we are on this amazing date and I'm bringing up my ex. Way to master the date, Heather."

"Hey." I stop just outside the restaurant and turn toward Heather. "He is the father of your son. And you had a marriage with him. This is your first foray into dating after all those years. I understand why he would come up. But now, he is insignificant. You have moved on and built a life for yourself. You manage a business and raise a child single-handedly. And you are the one who has captured my attention. His loss is my gain. And I am glad he is not here to see how foolish he was to let such a treasure of a woman slip away."

I nearly tell Heather she has captured not only my attention, but my heart, but our deadline makes me hold back the fullness of what I am feeling. If I express too much, it will only make it harder on both of us when I leave.

I hold the door to Harvested open and we step in together. The ambiance is perfect: low lighting, candles on every table, tasteful music filling the room. The hostess asks my name and then she seats us at the table I purposely reserved—one that gives us a view out onto the quaint main street of Harvest Hollow. The lamp posts are lit and twinkle lights span the street in a zig-zag formation, making the whole scene one that reminds me of the Christmas Markets back home.

We order our food and two glasses of wine.

I clasp Heather's hand in mine across the table. She smiles softly at me.

"Tell me about your home—in France."

"Oh! Are you ready for me to dominate the conversation now? Once I begin speaking of Avignon, I will find it hard to stop."

"I am ready." She rubs her thumb over mine.

"I wish I could take you there—to the city of the Popes."

"The city of the Popes?"

"It is our nickname. Not sexy, but important. Non?"

"Agreed. When I think of popes, I don't think of anything sexy." She laughs, and I join her.

"Our region, Provence-Alpes-Côte-d'Azur, includes Provence and the French Riviera as well as the Southernmost Alps. We are, of course, known for lavender fields, and our famous markets. But Avignon is a river city. We are on the Rhône. We have the Pope's Palace in the city. It is visited by tourists and loved by locals. Our theater and festivals are well known, as are our farmers markets and wonderful restaurants. Of course, we have many famous artists from our region. Van Gogh was only a half hour from Avignon in St. Remy. And Picasso painted the famous painting, *Les Demoiselles d'Avignon*, which we will not discuss tonight."

Heather's rapt attention is fixed on me so fully, and I am so swept up in the memories of each place and cultural treasure I am sharing with her, we barely notice the waiter arriving with our salads. He has to clear his throat.

Once he sets our plates down, I continue. "Many buildings are historical in Avignon. My flat is in a building from the fourteen hundreds."

"What? That's amazing."

"Also, it is why I do not step onto my balcony."

Heather laughs. And I stare shamelessly at the candlelight dancing in her eyes.

"But the best part of Avignon is the people. Especially my family. You would love them. You have met Pierre's family."

"I have. They are so sweet. It took a while for us to warm up to one another, but once we did, they have treated me like a long-lost sister."

"That is the way of many French. Sometimes we are formal and a little ... mmm ... closed off. But once we know you, we soften."

"You didn't seem to be closed off—ever." She laughs.

"Well, no man is his culture. We are each ourselves. I was born an ambassador, or so mon père told me."

"Your father?"

"Oui. Yes. My father. He would love you also."

"According to you, everyone would love me."

"And why not? What is not to love?"

She blushes and I raise my glass. She raises hers to meet mine. "To you, mon ange. May you always know what a treasure you are and never settle for less than you deserve."

Heather ducks her head and then she brings a finger to her face to swipe at a tear.

"Oh. No. Did I make you cry?"

"Good tears. No man has said anything like that to me—ever. And I know you mean it."

"I do. Of course I do. I only say what I mean."

She chuckles softly. "You say everything that comes into your head. No filter."

"This is mostly true."

"Mostly?"

"Maybe I hold back sometimes, when a beautiful, captivating woman is sitting across from me, and I know our time is short. But I only hold back what would rob us of this time together."

She smiles at me. Then she lifts our enjoined hands and kisses my knuckles reverently.

"You should come to France," I announce, once she releases my hand so she can eat.

"I wish I could. I haven't ever even been out of North Carolina."

"You are kidding me."

Heather looks shy. "Nope. Born and raised here."

"Well, you could do worse."

"I always wanted to travel—to see the world. But life sometimes throws you a curveball."

"A curveball?"

"In baseball, it's when the pitcher throws a ball the batter doesn't expect, so it curves. The batter swings at what he sees and he misses, or it goes totally off course from where he wanted it to go. We call unwanted detours in life, curveballs."

"That is a good saying." I reach for Heather again and stroke the top of her hand when she places it in mine. "A good saying, but not a good thing when you are the batter in life."

"Not always, no."

"Well, you must come. To France, that is."

"Maybe one day, I will."

The rest of dinner we talk about my childhood and hers, our favorite foods, dreams we have for our lives. The night passes at our table, through the main course, and then dessert, which we share, and I feed her a few bites from my fork. By the time I pay the check, we have been sitting together for over two hours.

"What would you like to do now?" I ask once we are standing on the sidewalk.

"Buy a ticket to France. Ask my parents to watch Nate for a few weeks. Leave Simon in charge of Catty, and tour all the places you described to me."

I smile at her, so tempted to pull out my phone and draw up the travel app. We both know she can't leave. The idea, though. What I wouldn't give to bring Heather home with me.

"One day, you will come."

I say the words even though there is no guarantee she will. And no guarantee we will both be single whenever she finally makes a trip overseas. I can't imagine Heather will be single for long. She has lowered her walls. Now she is open to romance. Any man could step in and fill this spot where I am standing.

My thoughts are tearing me up inside, so I clasp Heather's hand in mine and walk down Maple toward the car. I don't know where we will go, but I need to touch her and I need to move, to outrun the reality of our diminishing time together.

17

HEATHER

I'm wearing my favorite dress,
and the smile he gave me.

~ Unknown

I f denial were a sport, we'd be winning gold medals.
Rene and I walk hand in hand down Maple at a
leisurely pace, the scallops and steak and the chocolate cherry mousse cake all still fresh in my memory and on
my tastebuds. But nothing dominates my senses as much as
the thoughts scrolling through my mind: the way Rene
looked at me over dinner, the touch of his hand to mine, the
laughter we shared, the dreams I almost allowed myself to
indulge in.

I guess they're called dreams for a reason. At some point
you have to wake up and face reality.

We reach Pierre's car and Rene asks me again, "What
would you like to do now?"

"I would like to spend the night somewhere secluded, looking at the stars and talking until the sun comes up, kissing, you holding me."

I think Rene's starting to rub off on me. I'm blurting out every thought and feeling without a filter. He makes me bolder. He makes me a lot of things.

"We can find a place, Cher."

"I'm so sorry." I nearly pout. "I think I have to go to bed. I open in the morning. For now it's up to me every morning, but now that Adohi is starting on Monday, I will be able to take a few mornings a week off again."

"I'm glad," Rene says. "You need the time off. You have done so much. The shop survived this crisis because of your devotion. And now, it is time to give yourself a break."

"Bossy," I tease him.

"I am so very bossy. Do you hate it so much?"

I laugh. "Not so much."

"I will take you home. It is une tragédie."

"What is a tragedy?"

"I never took you dancing."

I look into his eyes. There are so many things we never did—things we will never do.

"Maybe," Rene says, turning so he is facing me. "We still can have one dance."

"Where?"

"Here?" He drags his hand down my arm until it meets my hand. With a firm, confident grip, he takes my hand. Then he lifts my other hand and places it on his shoulder. He lingers there, placing his palm over my knuckles and pressing my hand to his body. My eyes find his and he smiles that grin, full of warmth and want and always, always, a dash of impishness.

When he wraps his arm behind me and tugs me near, I almost forget where we are.

"Rene. There is no music."

"Shhh." He whispers in my ear.

And then he starts humming softly, his cheek grazing mine, his breath in my ear. He's swaying us on the sidewalk, right here on Maple in front of Pierre's car. I recognize the song a beat before he starts to sing, gently, into my hair, singing to me while he turns me and holds me in a private dance just for us.

I have never felt so light and simultaneously serious in my life. If I could hold on to any moment outside the day my son was born ... this. This is the one I want to package up, grasp on to, and keep forever.

When Rene stops singing, he gently slows our movements. He lifts a hand and brushes it down my hair. "I have forgotten something." His eyes search mine. "I never asked you to be my Valentine."

"Mmmm."

"Will you?"

"Be your Valentine?"

"Yes, Cher. It may be the only time in my life I ask a woman that question, and I'm asking you tonight."

His statement is too much, but I feel it too. How will we ever find this again anywhere, on any continent? I'm old enough to know how rare this kind of connection is. I don't date because I've eliminated all the options already. No one is worth the effort or what it would mean to bring them into Nate's life. Rene is. He's different from anyone I've known. What we have found between us is rare.

"I will. I'll be your Valentine."

"And that means, I am yours."

If only he were.

Rene leans in then, and places a soft kiss on my lips, cupping my cheek with his hand. He doesn't prolong this kiss. He places another gentle brush of his lips on my nose and then he holds me to himself in an embrace that feels like so much more than a hug.

Without a word, he turns, and with his arm around my shoulder, walks me to the passenger side of Pierre's car.

When we are both buckled, I turn to Rene. "Are we foolish not to think of what happens after this?"

His answer is swift. "No."

"No?"

"We are the wisest people. Fools would ruin this perfect week with thoughts of what's to come. We are wise enough to cherish what we have."

I'm quiet. Rene reaches over and clasps my hand. Even this gesture has started to feel so familiar. How will it be when he's gone and no one grabs my hand when I need assurance?

It will be like it's always been. My old normal will be my life again. I was fine before he came here. I'll be fine when he returns to France. At least, that's what I'm telling myself.

My brain has started rolling and it's like a boulder going downhill. I can't stop thinking of what things will be like now that I've started obsessing on our inevitable separation.

"But what will it be like when you visit again?"

"I will be so happy to see you. And you will be thrilled, so very happy you will not be able to contain your joy. You will almost squeal with delight at the sight of me."

I laugh.

Rene's voice grows serious. "We don't know what it will be like, Cher. How could we? Does anyone really know? If our lives were different, we would be together. I would be taking you on many more dates, and we would be deciding how serious this thing between us will become. But our lives are not those lives. We are two paths who converged in a beautiful clearing and soon will head in separate directions. Let's enjoy this shared space while we are here. And when I see you again, even if you are in the arms of another man, I will smile, remembering what we have shared."

I will never be in the arms of another man. I can't say those words to him—it's too soon. But I know with everything I am that this, what I've found with Rene, is something I will never find again. And if I can't have it with him, I will just keep the memories and see him whenever he visits.

Rene pulls into my driveway and kills the engine. We walk toward my porch and he pulls me into a kiss. I lean in, holding on to the lapels of his coat as if I could keep him here through sheer willpower. We kiss for a few minutes, murmuring sweet words to one another with our foreheads resting together afterward. Rene brushes the back of his hand down my cheek when we pull apart.

"Thank you for being my Valentine, Cher."

"Thank you. I will never forget this night."

He smiles down at me and then he lets me go. I open my home, walk in and shut the door behind me, fighting the urge to turn around and ask him for one more kiss, one more hug, one more of anything he has to give me before he leaves.

THE NEXT MORNING, I open the shop alone. Rene shows up fifteen minutes later than he has the whole past week and I have to wonder if he is intentionally weaning us off one another. If he is, it is a kindness, helping us ease into what is coming in four days.

Simon arrives at seven, buffering the odd tension in the room, and then the morning crowd descends in full force and we are mercifully distracted from anything but serving customers for a few hours.

It's around eleven when my phone rings. It's Melanie.

"Hey." I instinctively walk through the swinging door toward my office.

She never calls.

"Oh, Heather. We just got wind of the employee situation. I wish you would have called us."

"I handled it. I didn't want to worry you. Handling employee schedules and call-offs comes with the territory of being a manager, right?"

"Two employees quitting on the same day comes with ownership of a small business, but you've spared us most of that sort of reality for several years now. Stan and I can't thank you enough. Your next paycheck will have a hefty bonus to reflect our gratitude."

"Oh. You don't have to ..."

"We most definitely do, and I want you to tell us if anything like this happens in the future."

The future. Are they keeping the shop? My heart lifts at the thought.

"And that's what I'm calling you about."

I'm quiet, waiting to hear whatever Melanie's about to say.

"The couple you met when we came in, Garrett and Livvy?"

"Mm hmm." A numbness seeps through me, causing my mind to feel fuzzy.

"They are making an offer on the property."

"On the property."

"I probably should have called you when you weren't at the shop. I just figured this time of day there's a lull. Did I catch you when you're busy?"

"No. No. I'm fine. You hit the lull."

I'm dying to ask Melanie if they are keeping Cataloochee open or planning to put a different business here, but I can't get the words out. Rene shows up in the office doorway. His brow draws in as soon as he sees me. My dread must be written all over my face. Without a moment's hesitation, he steps into the small room with me and places his hand on my shoulder. Our eyes lock and I'm anchored like a ship in the storm who has found her safe harbor.

"We're just in the early stages. But the offer is in. These things take months."

Months.

Melanie's words blur. She says something about thirty days of due diligence, followed by a few months waiting for the financing contingencies to be worked out and then two weeks for something else. I can't focus on facts. This one word keeps ricocheting through my brain: *months. Months. Months.*

And this whole time, Rene's gentle grip on my shoulder keeps me from crumbling.

"We'll keep you posted, Heather. And we're so grateful for you. Without you, Stan and I wouldn't be in this position. You've been a godsend."

"I love it here." I manage to get the sentence out without the crack in my voice sounding too noticeable.

"Okay, well, have a great rest of your day."

"You too."

I click end and look up at Rene.

"Talk to me, Cher. What was that about?"

"The sale. Melanie and Stan found buyers for the property."

"For the shop?"

"Yes. She said something about months. I should have taken notes. I'm just ..."

"In shock." He finishes my sentence for me.

Then he drops to a squatting position in front of me, bracing his hands on my thighs and looking up into my eyes.

"I'm sorry, Cher. So sorry."

He doesn't try to fix me or tell me everything will be alright. He just stays there, holding my gaze, settling me with his wordless presence until something in me—a small, almost imperceptible voice—tells me I will make it—no matter what happens.

"Thank you." I let out a shuddery breath.

"I didn't do anything."

"You were here when I needed you. I didn't have to process that call that alone."

"You never do." Rene's face is serious, partly in that bossy, take-charge mode he drifts into at times. It seems those are the times I need to borrow from his strength most.

"Did they say what will happen? Is this going to be a transfer of business or merely property?"

"She didn't say. And I didn't ask."

"Okay."

Again, he doesn't push me. Other men would tell me I should have asked, after all, my future hangs in the balance here—and Nate's. But Rene trusts me. He knows I'll find out everything I need to know in due time. Maybe this one chunk of reality is all I can handle for today. More will come —sooner than later, unfortunately.

"My experience ... do you want to hear it?"

"Yes, please."

"My experience is that these types of deals have many components. They can fall apart at any time. The buyers have to qualify, much like a home purchase. And there are many other details when it is a purchase of a commercial property as that impacts a community as well. Nothing is final until the keys are in the buyer's hands."

I breathe out a breath I didn't know I was holding.

"Right. I'll just take this one thing at a time."

"And move to France and open a cafe?"

"Exactly. That was my next sentence. You beat me to it."

We both laugh. It feels good to lighten up a little—leave it to Rene to lead me into a headspace with less doomsday and more hope. He always seems to do that.

He draws me into a hug and I collapse into the strength and comfort of his arms. He brushes his hand in reassuring strokes up and down my back and I cling to him—even though I should be practicing letting go.

18

HEATHER

The scary thing about distance is
you don't know whether
they'll miss you or forget you.
~ Nicholas Sparks

"Heather, it's like you aren't even here with us."
Tasha's voice is tinged with a sisterly cocktail of
concern and irritation.

Hannah, Tasha and I are sitting around in Tasha's living
room on the floor around the coffee table. Tasha made three
pots of fondue—two cheeses and one chocolate—and she's
got plates scattered between with chunks of fruit, veggies
and bread for dipping. I haven't really been eating.

"Go easy on her," Hannah says. "This is Rene's last night
in town and she doesn't even get to spend it with him
because he's out with Pierre for some quality guy time. You
can't blame her for being a tad distracted."

"I don't. Not at all. I get it." Tasha looks at me. "Sorry, Heath. I just hate seeing you like this. It was the very thing Pierre worried about when Rene first showed up."

"Pierre worried about Rene sweeping me off my feet and then leaving me here with a broken heart?"

Tasha's eyes go wide. I haven't spelled my feelings out so clearly before tonight.

"No. Pierre worried Rene would try to flirt, and you would feel pestered by him."

I chuckle, remembering how I felt when Rene first showed up in Harvest Hollow for this visit.

"I would have never imagined ..." I say, shaking my head.

"There's no way to predict who we'll fall for and when. Look at me and Pierre."

"True."

"How did last night go?" Hannah asks. She spears a chunk of sourdough and dips it into the Swiss fondue.

"It was fun. I mean those two ... they both are such hams."

Nate and I made dinner for Rene last night. The three of us hung out watching Nate's favorite movie, *Home Alone*. When Nate heard that Rene had never seen it, he insisted on hosting a movie night. Rene laughed so loud anytime one of the bad guys got injured, he even snorted a few times. I think I watched Rene far more than I kept my eyes on the screen.

Tonight, Nate is with my parents. Rene and Pierre are spending the evening together. They haven't had as much time together as they had planned this trip—partly because Pierre's unexpected inspiration spurred him to get a jump on writing this next novel, and mostly because Rene was helping me at the shop.

"I'm sorry I'm not the best company tonight. I promise I will be. Give me a week or two."

"A week or two?" Hannah gives me a side eye.

"I'll be back to normal soon. Tonight's just hard. I want Pierre and Rene to have time together, but I can't help feeling greedy for every spare minute with Rene before he leaves. I guess this is just good practice. I'm getting a head start on getting over him."

"You and Rene." Tasha shakes her head. "I never would have won that bet. And I'm glad. He's been good for you."

"So good," I agree. "But let's change the subject."

Hannah and Tasha look at one another like there's no other topic in the world more interesting than my inability to choose an available man. First, I picked Andrew who couldn't be faithful, and then I picked a kind, funny, devoted man who lives over four thousand miles away. Go me.

The sound of a car engine pulling into the driveway catches our attention. I can't help the flutter of my heart, hoping it's Rene and Pierre. It can't be. They only left an hour ago.

"Are you expecting anyone?" Hannah asks Tasha.

"No."

The door opens and in walks Rene, followed by Pierre. My face lights up like the Christmas tree in the town square.

Pierre has a smirk on his face. "Someone was the worst company in the history of any friendship since Cesar and Brutus. So pouty."

Rene looks sheepish.

"Was something bothering you?" Tasha teases Rene.

Hannah discretely reaches over and squeezes my knee. I'm smiling like a big goof.

"He kept talking about your sister," Pierre says to Tasha.

"So I suggested we join you. I've never seen a man push a chair away from a table more quickly."

Rene's looking at me like he's guilty as charged, but there's a warmth between us, and I feel settled now that he's here. This is bad. Very bad. But also, so good. I never thought I could feel like this.

"Hi, Heather." Rene's trademark laser focus makes me feel like we're the only two people here.

"Hello."

"Well, come in, you two," Hannah says, breaking the spell. "I'll be the fifth wheel—but only because Tasha made my favorite fondue."

The three of us women are cross-legged on the floor. Rene takes a seat on the couch behind me and tugs my shoulders back. I recline between his legs while I make him a plate of fondue.

The five of us talk and eat for the next few hours until it's time for me to leave so I can open at Catty tomorrow morning. Rene walks me out after Hannah takes off.

"I'm glad you came back," I tell him.

"Me too. It is tellement pathétique how much I missed you."

"Pathetic?"

"Oui." He brushes his hand along my hair. "Maybe you will learn French."

"I can guarantee you I won't. I took Spanish in high school and butchered that language so badly, I had to take a makeup class over the summer. Languages are not my thing."

When I stop speaking, I look at Rene. There's a dejected look in his eyes that mirrors my own heart. I won't learn his language, which solidifies the fact that I won't be moving to his country—not that a move like that was ever on the table.

"I mean. I could try to learn."

"Oui. Just un peu." He holds his fingers up in a pinch.

"A little?"

"See. You are not hopeless, Cher."

"I feel pretty hopeless," I confess.

Rene steps into my space, brushing his hand down my face and leaving his hand resting on my cheek. "Me too. I feel it. But feelings are like weather. They come and they blow away. What is here ..." He places his hand over my heart. "Will weather all the storms."

I don't ask Rene anything. I don't ask him to stay. Definitely not to relocate. Not even to consider the future. He leaves in fewer than twenty-four hours. Right now, he's here.

He lifts my hand to his mouth and then he starts kissing the inside of my wrist, down to my palm, and then over each fingertip. Every so often, he lifts his eyes to meet mine, and I'm going to need someone to find a human-sized spatula to scrape the melted puddle of goo I've become off the driveway.

Frenchmen. It's the French thing. I'm sure of it.

No. It's not.

It's Rene. It's him. He's it, the one my heart has been waiting for. And he lives an ocean away in a country he loves, with a career he's been working hard at for years—his own real estate business. He is the primary agent.

I'm a single mom managing a local coffee shop with an eight-year-old who needs my feet on the ground, not my head in the clouds.

But Rene keeps going, tugging me near, placing soft

kisses along my cheek and then my neck, murmuring words in French and English.

Mon ange.

You are everything I never knew I needed.

Oh, I will miss you.

Que ferai-je sans toi?

I don't ask for translations. I close my eyes and soak in Rene's attentive devotion. He trails kisses along my jaw and claims my mouth in a kiss that says everything.

This is our goodbye.

Yes. Nate and I will take off school and work early to see Rene off at the airport tomorrow with Pierre and Tasha, but we will be in a crowd. These are the last few moments the two of us will have alone together during Rene's trip.

I lean in, running my hands through his hair, gripping his shoulders, melting into him. And then we separate, and he holds me, lightly swaying the way a parent soothes their bereft child, only it's us he's consoling.

When Rene pulls back to look me in the eyes, he says, "I have joked about this, but I am serious right now. If you could take some time, come visit Avignon? Maybe you would fall in love—with France."

"I'm sure I would fall in love—with France. And ..."

Rene shakes his head. "I know. You can't. Nate's life is here. He has lived through enough loss and change in his short life."

"You could ..." I start to offer an alternative.

"Move to the states?"

"It's silly. Forget I said it."

"My life is in France—my responsibilities, my family, my business. Your life is here with the shop and your son and your family. Our hearts will have to be content floating together somewhere over the ocean between our two homes."

THE NEXT DAY, I leave Simon in charge so I can pick Nate up from school a few hours early. Rene is flying out of Asheville, which is nearly an hour away. The five of us will drive together. Rene and I never told Nate we were more than friends. There really was no reason to give Nate such a big issue to process when nothing will come of Rene's and my feelings for one another.

Tasha and Pierre are up in the front seat. Nate is buckled in between Rene and me, and he's chattering away one hundred miles an hour about making the little league softball team.

"I'm gonna hit that ball like I'm smackin' a watermelon."

I shake my head. My son has never smacked a watermelon.

"That sounds messy." Pierre smiles at Nate, and Nate beams up at him.

"It's gonna be messy for the other team. We're gonna cream them. I already practiced with my grandpa in the backyard. Didn't I, Mom?"

"You did."

"I wish you could see my games, Mister Rene. Do they have fun things like baseball in France?"

"We have a little baseball, but we really like football. You call it soccer here."

"Wait! You call football, soccer? That's just weird."

"We call football like you have, American football. We call soccer, football."

Nate makes a circling motion next to his head with his pointer finger. "That's coo coo."

Rene continues smiling down at Nate. And I smile at the ease the two of them have always shared. They are the same species—lovers of life, fearless, secretly hiding very sensitive hearts under the surface. I wish I had seen that about Rene sooner. I wouldn't have wasted so much time pushing him away.

Rene's arm sneaks over behind my son's head and he gives my shoulder a reassuring squeeze.

"Maybe your mom can film some of your games and send me videos."

It's the first time either of us has spoken of staying in touch in any way aside from the times Rene comes here for visits, and even then we've left the future wide open.

"I can do that."

"I look forward to seeing you smash those baseballs," Rene says to Nate.

Nate beams. There's something magical about a man encouraging the boy who has been raised around mostly women. It hits a spot none of us can reach, no matter how hard we try. Nate has a good life. His relationship with Rene has filled in some gaps—even if only for a short few weeks.

We get to the airport far too quickly. This day is slipping away like sand through my fingertips.

Rene lifts his bags from the trunk at the curb. Nate and I walk into the terminal with him while Tasha and Pierre park the car. We won't kiss goodbye. I already feel his absence as if he's a hologram of himself.

After Rene checks his bags, the three of us stand in a spot off to the side of the airline counters, awkwardly waiting for Tasha and Pierre. Rene catches my eyes several times and smiles at me. I smile back, always aware of Nate and the impression our interactions are making on him.

Pierre and Tasha show up, and now there's only an hour and a half until Rene flies away. I have thousands of things I want to say to him and one kiss I wish I could share. One, and then another ... and another.

I gave myself a good long pep talk before bed last night, reminding myself that the whole reason I am staying in Harvest Hollow and not pursuing Rene is Nate. And Nate's highest good has always been the worthiest reason for sacrificing any freedom or desires.

Knowing I'm doing this for Nate gives me a willingness and sense of purpose that tempers my grief. I look down at my son. He's chatting away with Rene about things in France.

"But you do have ice cream?"

"Oui. We have very good ice cream. We call it glace."

"What? Why do you have to make new names for everything? That probably gets really confusing. You could just call it ice cream. You know? By its real name?"

Rene chuckles. "Did you know France is older than America?"

Nate shakes his head.

"We named things first."

"Ohhh. So, why don't we call it glace?"

"That is an excellent question." Rene winks at me, and I try not to shed a tear.

"Can I come have glace with you sometime?"

"It's really far to France, Nater." *So. So. Far.* It may as well be the moon.

"I knooooow, Mom. But we could fly, like Mister Rene is doing."

"We could."

"Maybe," Rene says very diplomatically. "We will see. We don't want you to miss any baseball games. Your team needs you here. But you are always welcome."

Nate smiles.

Pierre announces, "It's probably time."

Rene nods and steps into Pierre's embrace. They don't hug and slap one another like a lot of American men. They hold onto one another and whatever shred of my heart didn't belong to Rene surrenders and I fall just a little further for this man who is all heart.

Then Rene steps in front of Tasha. "Take care of my best friend and my nephew."

"We don't know if it's a boy."

"And that is not my decision. We could all know if you would check. Either way, I will be back when your baby is here."

He looks over at me. It's a promise. I will see him again, but it won't matter because he will always have to leave.

Tasha reaches out and she and Rene hug.

Next, Rene moves to Nate.

"You're not going to kiss me, are you?" my son asks with a wary look on his face.

"No. Just a hug if you'll let me."

"Okay."

They hug and I watch Nate's hands fist the back of Rene's shirt. How I hold it together is beyond me.

"Let's go see if this airport has ice cream," Pierre says to Nate, catching me off guard.

"I don't think they do, Uncle Pierre."

"Let's make sure. If they don't we can stop on the way home."

"Really?" Nate turns to me. "Can we, Mom?"

I'd buy Nate an ice cream truck at this point. Pierre is a genius.

"Yes. Sure."

Nate and Pierre walk away and Tasha smiles over at me before joining them.

"I didn't think we'd have time alone."

"I asked Pierre to take care of that." Rene's eyes soften.

"You think of everything."

"If that were true, Cher, I would think of a way for us to be together."

I nod and Rene steps toward me. I think he's going to kiss me, but he pulls me into a hug instead and I melt into his arms, holding on this one last time. We stand like that, two people clinging to one another, while the rest of the passengers and employees mill around us. Thankfully, tearful goodbyes are common sights at airports.

"There are many things I want to tell you, Heather. But I want you to know you have made your way deep into my heart, into a place no one has owned before. And you will now own that spot forever. It is yours alone."

He isn't saying he loves me, but he may as well be.

"I ... you are in my heart too."

"I know, Cher. I know."

And he does know. Somehow, this man who seemed so self-absorbed and superficial turned out to be the most attentive, perceptive person I've known.

"Mon cœur." Rene moves toward me, cupping my jaw.

I tilt my head up to meet him. He brushes the softest kiss over my lips, letting his lips linger there for the sweetest moment. Our connection is tender and full of emotion. He could kiss me one hundred ways, but this one is perfect.

Then he draws me back into his arms and holds me again. Inevitably, he draws back.

"I need to catch my plane. You never know with security. Last time a woman had a box of chocolat shaped like actual human bones. Security thought the bones were as real as they appeared in the X-ray. Everything went from routine to alert in one second. The agent let out a gasp. The woman was held by two guards. We all had to wait while her candy was inspected."

I chuckle.

Rene's eyes are soft. "I will miss you, mon ange."

"I will miss you too."

Rene leans in and kisses my forehead. And then he steps backward, still holding my gaze. I memorize this moment, the green of his eyes, the wave of his hair, the firm and kind tone in his voice, his beautiful accent, the tug of longing between us.

"Be good to yourself."

I nod and swipe at one rogue tear that refused to wait for a more opportune time to make its escape down my cheek.

"You too."

Rene stoops to grab his carry-on satchel and then he loops it over his shoulder. I stand still watching him. And then Pierre, Tasha and Nate show up. Nate's got a bag of candy in his hand.

"We couldn't find ice cream, so I got candy!" my son shouts loud enough that the workers on the tarmac probably hear him.

Then he turns to Rene and says, "No glace."

Rene beams at Nate. Then he waves at all of us and turns. The four of us watch him walk away until he turns a corner and is out of sight.

19

RENE

If I miss you any harder,
my heart might come looking for you.
~ Gemma Troy

M y neighbor's nighttime noises filter through the walls, accentuating my loneliness. The day I returned to Avignon, I texted Pierre and Heather separately.

To Pierre, I said, *I made it. Thank you for the visit.*

To Heather, I said, *I am safely home, but my heart remains in North Carolina. Take good care of it, since it is yours.*

Am I being overly-dramatic and a cliché romantic? Maybe.

I saw my family the first weekend after my return. They do not understand my new affection for America. When I speak to Pierre on the phone he teases me, saying things like,

"Oh, how the mighty fall." But then he commiserates with my plight. After all, he stood at this same crossroads only a few years ago, deciding whether to move to America for the woman he loved.

Had I known how excruciating it would feel to return home, I might have decided to take a risk and stay. I am here in body, but not in heart. During the three weeks since my return, I have closed two sales. Business is as good as ever. I went out with local friends a few nights during the first week after I came home. I am terrible company. I have declined several invitations to drinks or to go dancing since then. Staying home doesn't help. Going out doesn't help. Working barely takes the edge off. I am a man caught in a situation that seems to have no way out.

Heather has sent me a few videos of Nate playing base-ball. Her texts are formal and kind. She will say, *Miss you.* But nothing more. It is a good thing I know her. She only allows herself to feel a fraction of her emotions, and expresses even fewer than she acknowledges. Then she tucks the rest away so she can fulfill her responsibilities. Sometimes I want to push her into admitting how desperately she misses me—in the same way I miss her. But I know she is preserving herself and doing what is needed. So, I force myself to accept what we are now—two people who fell for one another and had to move on.

My phone rings as I am getting ready for bed. Pierre.

"Allo?"

"Allo. Bonne soirée. Comment allez-vous?"

"You know how I am doing. Business is better than ever. And I am a shell of a man."

"You could move to America."

Usually Pierre is not so bold. That is my job—to always speak my mind. It comes naturally to me, whereas Pierre is more reserved. He takes his time before sharing whatever he has been considering. Often, I need to drag his thoughts out of him.

"I don't think I can. I'm not like you. More than anything, I am a Frenchman. I belong in France."

The words feel less convincing than they used to.

"You belong where your heart is."

Again, with the boldness. Maybe his confrontation is what I need.

"We are at an impasse. Heather and I shared a few lovely weeks—perhaps the best weeks of my life. Let's chalk it up to that. In time, I will adjust. Spring is around the corner. I will go into the country. That has always restored me."

"I don't think a trip to the country will heal you this time. But we will see."

"How is Heather?"

I ask him about her every time we talk, and he refuses to tell me. Usually he says, *ask her yourself.*

"She is like a woman whose heart has flown away."

Hearing what I already suspected feels like a punch to my sternum. She is miserable too? I might be able to endure my own misery, but I can't stomach the thought of hers.

"That is too much for me to bear," I confess to Pierre.

"Oui. It should be. Especially when you are the only one who can make this better. I know it is a complicated decision. You have to think of Nate ... and your business. Life here is not France. There are many beautiful sights and the people are kind. But you will miss the croissants and the coffee, the historic buildings, our language. You will forever feel like you are visiting another country like a nomad. Something will always call you home. You will live the life of a man divided."

"That's not a sales pitch. You may need to work on your presentation."

"I'm being honest with you, mon ami. Choosing to live in a foreign country is not easy. I did not come here and feel it was the home I have been meant to find. I miss France. But my life is here because Tasha is here, and she is now my life. And, as for you, what is the life you have now? You are already torn between two continents. That will never change."

"I might have fallen in love in America," I confess. "Even if I didn't fall in love with America."

"Might?"

"I did. I love Heather. Are you happy now?"

Pierre chuckles. "Why would I be happy when my friend is being an idiot? If you fell in love, why aren't you here? What is left in France for you now?"

"My career. My business. My family. My community. My roots."

"Hmmm."

"So, I should simply fly back to America and declare my love like one of those men in your books?"

"They are best sellers for a reason."

"You are of no help."

"I'm not saying you should be foolish. But maybe ... tell Heather how you feel. Or better yet, show her."

"Show her? How will I show her?"

"You are the one always parading around about how we Frenchmen have the monopoly on love and romance. I'm sure you'll think of something. And I'm looking forward to having you nearby."

"You are, are you? How are you so sure I will end up in North Carolina?"

"I'd bet my next advance on it."

20

HEATHER

When we kissed for the first time,
I could swear that I heard our souls whisper,
ever so quietly, "Welcome home."
~ Beau Taplin

My days off are the worst. Tasha and Pierre make sure I take time away from Cataloochee, but I don't know what to do with myself while Nate is at school and the shop doesn't need me. The sale is going through to the new owners, and Melanie and Stan are tight lipped about whether the coffee shop will have a future. Melanie says she'll tell me as soon as she's allowed to disclose the details. Rumor has it the new owners may want to change things to include a trendy bistro feel to appeal to the younger adults in town. The location is prime.

I have dreams—actual dreams while I'm sleeping—of a crowd of our regulars standing in front of the door to the shop, arms outstretched, refusing the new owners entrance. Of course, that won't happen. Our town loves our staple shops, but we also go gaga over new stores and restaurants.

When it comes down to it, Floyd might be the only one standing beside me in an effort to hang on to Catty.

My stir-craziness hit a fevered pitch this morning. I was sitting on the couch Googling translations of various English words into French, like the pathetic woman I have become. I still won't ever really learn the language. I don't catch on to foreign languages easily. So this smattered collection of random phrases is basically useless. My heart is a jumbled mess.

I finally pack myself up and drive to Tasha's. Pierre is deep into writing mode now. His body's on the couch, head bent over his laptop, but his mind is somewhere in France, creating a fictional romance set somewhere in the country of his birth. I've never had more in common with my brother-in-law than I do now.

"So," Tasha asks me. "Why don't you go visit? You never take time off. Adohi and Simon are doing great. I could check in on the shop every morning and evening while you're gone. Even Melanie has said she wants you to pull her and Stan in on things more than you have in the past. Between all of us, you could take a week and go to France. Nate could stay here or with Mom and Dad."

We're in the kitchen, at her table. I'm nursing a coffee while she sips herbal tea and shifts around in the chair trying to find a comfortable position with her ever-growing abdomen.

"What good would a visit do me? I would see Rene, fall more deeply in love, and still have to come home to a life without him."

"True. It's not fair. I'm so, so sorry."

"It was too much. I should have never let you, and Nate, and Rene ... and our parents ... our parents, Tasha! I let all of you conspire to make me open up and feel, and now look at me. I felt it all."

It's not their fault, I know. But grief loves a convenient target.

"I know." Tasha places her hand over mine. "I really had this idea that somehow he'd choose to stay here. It's never an easy decision, but the way he looked at you? The depth of your connection? I was sure he'd stay."

"It was like nothing I ever imagined. *He* is like no one I've ever known. He just—gets me. When he would kiss that tender skin inside my wrist and the place right here." I point to my neck. "And place his hand here?" My hand lands on my heart and I sob. One big gulp of a sob.

I look into Tasha's eyes with a plea, as if she could change all of this for me.

Then I take a cleansing breath in through my nose and hold it while I straighten my spine and my resolve. When I breathe out it's like I'm releasing everything: Rene, my feelings, the longing for more. I have a good life. I love this town, my family, my son, and my coffee shop, even though it's not mine, and even though it may be closing in a few months.

Tasha is staring at me, wide eyed. Then she narrows her gaze. "You did that thing again."

"What thing?"

"That thing where you breathe deeply and grab up your inner resources and gird yourself against the world. Only, Heather, no one here is trying to harm you. We all love you. Even Rene."

"I love him too," I cave, permitting all my grief to come flooding back with those short four words.

We've never said that we love one another, time and circumstances never gave us the chance.

Tasha stares at me. "You're allowed to fall for a man, you know?"

"I know. Of course. Yeah. I know—in theory."

My relentless sister presses on. "It's not like you need to stay single for Nate."

"I'm not. If Rene were here, I would open up the floodgates. I really wanted to give him a chance—the whole chance, no holding back."

Tasha looks me in the eye in the way only a sister can. "You are an amazing mom."

I nod, unable to form words. My throat feels tight. I don't know what me being an amazing mom has to do with my love life, but the fact that she affirms it right now has me choking on the already overwhelming emotions that have been brewing in me for weeks now—ever since Rene boarded his plane and returned to France.

"And you're also a woman. A brilliant, funny, amazing woman." Tasha pauses. Then she carefully says, "One day, Nate will grow up and move on."

I shake my head as if I can shake off the reality of Nate growing up and leaving me alone. I think of his future daily, but to hear Tasha say it out loud makes it too real.

"It's ... you don't understand."

"What don't I understand?"

"I'm that girl."

"What girl?"

"The cliché. The one who fell hard—for Andrew. I believed him. I gave myself over to him completely and got pregnant with his child. And then, one day, I walked in on him with another woman—the younger woman with a body that hadn't given birth and stayed up nights nursing."

Tasha isn't fazed by anything I'm saying. She lived through it all. "Oh my gosh. Do you hear yourself?" She straightens her back and sits upright. "You have *nothing* to do with the choices that man made. He had a treasure in his hands and he crapped all over it. The best two people I know, besides Pierre, are you and Nate. That guy who married you made vows. He took all he had been freely given and tossed it away carelessly. That has nothing to do with you. *Nothing*."

I shake my head. She doesn't get it. I love her fiercely defending me. She always will.

"It has everything to do with me, though. I picked him. I didn't see what he was capable of. I should have seen it. I guess what they say is true. Love is blind."

"Well, if we go with that logic, I was blind too. I'm just as much at fault. And I wasn't in love. You think I would have let you commit to a man I thought was going to rip through your trust and your heart and shred everything you were building together over a fling?"

"It wasn't a fling. They're still together."

The fact of Andrew's current relationship status is irrelevant. I don't even know if I loved Andrew—not after experiencing what I did with Rene. What Rene and I shared in a few short weeks surpassed years of anything I shared with Andrew.

Tasha gives a light shake of her head. "Heather, you know me. I watch for things. You couldn't have known Andrew was capable of what he did. None of us saw his infidelity coming. And what does Andrew have to do with your current predicament anyway?"

"Nothing. But I do. I'm the common denominator. I pick unavailable men."

Tasha tilts her head so she's looking askance at me and then she pinches her lips together.

Finally, she says. "I just want you to be happy."

"I'm happy," I manage to whisper out. "It's just ... Rene made me want to be reckless—to run barefoot through wild fields of lavender and leisurely sip a cappuccino at a table on some cobblestone patio outside a cafe. I want to breathe him in and nestle in his arms and relax and let go of the side of me that's always making lists and keeping track and drawing lines and making sure the shelves are stocked.

"I want to rest in his playful assurance that life isn't meant to be taken so seriously. I want to stare into his gorgeous green eyes and lose myself in his kisses. And all those things would be mine in some other life—in a life where I hadn't married the wrong man and walked away from that marriage with the most amazing child who needs me to be both mom and dad to him. Maybe I was too reckless, starting something I knew Rene and I couldn't finish."

Tasha smiles softly. "I said Rene was good for you. And he was. You never would have said anything like *run barefoot through wild fields of lavender* before his visit." She giggles.

"Because those fields are probably all prickery in real life. The idea of dashing through those fields isn't reality. Just like my feelings for Rene. They are dreamy and impractical. Full of sharp splinters."

Tasha literally rolls her eyes. Then she softens her expression. "I think the two of you haven't written your last chapter.

You're still in the middle of the book. Things are always a mess in the middle. It looks like nothing will work out, but then ... it does. And you'll get your happily ever after."

"I never, ever believed in those. For good reason."

"I know."

"I'm glad you got yours, though. You and Pierre deserve all this and more."

"And so do you, Heath."

"Maybe. But I don't think I'm the happily-ever-after type. Some of us just have to work harder at everything. And then we get a really good life, but it's always a bit lumpy and precarious."

Tasha doesn't even have an opportunity to contradict me with any of her pie-in-the-sky perspective because my phone rings. It's Melanie.

"Heather?"

"Yes."

"I'm so glad I caught you."

"Is everything okay? I'm at Tasha's but I can come in to the shop. I can be there in ten minutes."

"Everything's fine. The shop is fine, I imagine. I just need to tell you, there's been a turn of events with the sale."

"Oh?"

I practically hold my breath. Tasha looks over at me with a questioning expression.

"The buyers had to drop out."

"Oh." I breathe out my breath, hoping my relief doesn't carry across the phone line.

"We're still selling. And, Mark already has a buyer. This new buyer was adamant that the space remain Cataloochee Mountain Coffee and that you stay on as manager. He wrote both those contingencies into the contract. We'll keep you posted. He's coming for a walk-through next week, so you'll get to meet him in person."

"Oh."

That one syllable seems to be the extent of my vocabulary now. Oh. Oh. Oh. I'm like Santa, only less jolly.

"It's a lot to take in, but honestly, Stan and I feel so much better about this buyer. I think you will too. The terms are certainly more comforting. We never could force someone to keep the shop open, after all, we're abandoning shop." She laughs lightly. "Like abandoning ship! Get it?" She laughs a little more and I smile. "But we're so glad the new buyer wants to keep everything the same."

"Me too," I manage to say.

"We'll keep you posted. Enjoy the rest of your day. Sorry to have interrupted. I just had to tell you."

"Thank you. I really appreciate it."

I hang up with Melanie and look over at Tasha.

"What was all that about?"

"The buyers dropped out of the sale of Cataloochee. But there's a new buyer. He's touring next week. At least he wants to keep the shop open. He won't be changing anything. He even said he still wants me on as manager." I pause. "I wonder who it could be."

"Wouldn't it be crazy if it were Rene?"

Tasha's face is alight with possibility.

"Crazy is the operative word there. He's in France. He's not buying a coffee shop in America. Could he even afford that? Not that he would."

"He can afford it. He's made a lot in real estate. He doesn't just sell properties. He owns a bunch of rentals, and he buys homes and has crews fix them up for resale. He's quite the businessman."

"I never knew."

"How much talking did the two of you do?" Tasha's brows wiggle.

"We talked plenty, gutter-brain."

She laughs. "And he kissed you here." She touches my wrist lightly. "And here." She reaches over and touches my neck. "And here." She lightly taps my lips. "It's not over between you two. That's all I know."

"Stop filling my tank with hope. I need to grieve."

"Yeah. Let me let you get back to that."

"Besides, wouldn't Rene tell Pierre—tell all of us—if he were buying a coffee shop—my coffee shop?"

"Probably. I just enjoy dreaming."

"Understatement." I smile at my sister. Even though my reality hasn't changed, being with her did lighten my mood for the time being.

21

HEATHER

In the end, I'll always come running back to you,
not because I'm weak,
but because I fell in love with you.
~ Unknown

I 'm adjusting. That's probably the best word for whatever happens to a person over time when they have no choice but to adapt to a situation that isn't their choosing.

I make a round through Catty, smiling at customers, picking up dishes, walking into the back to deposit my collection near the sink. Simon is on shift with me. But he's on break, reading a book on the front couch and eating a pastry. The morning crowd has thinned, and as happens most days, I hear Rene's kind voice like a ghost whisper, asking me if I ate, or telling me to take a break before the lunch rush. He only worked in the shop for less than two weeks, but his presence made him feel like a fixture—and not only in the shop. As I predicted, time has helped me ease back into my routine. It's been over a month and a half since Rene left. Spring has sprung in our town. The tulips are out in my front yard, the wildflowers cover the local mountains, days are longer, and customers are talking about heading to the Dreamville concert in Raleigh this coming weekend.

It's all a reminder that life has its seasons and, like my tulips, what feels dead and hopeless can come to life again against all appearances that say otherwise.

I sent Rene a few more videos of Nate's baseball games, but nothing else. I know better than to dabble in a long-distance texting exchange that leads to more heartache. Sometimes a clean break is the kindest decision. Rene always sends back something like "Wow! Look at Nate! He's a star!" or "Great hit! Look at Nate go." Nothing about us.

It's like he knows how much I can handle. I'm sure he does. No one has ever read me like Rene. He had this uncanny knack for seeing behind my defenses and walls and really knowing my heart and mind even though I attempted to keep it partially guarded.

The bell over the door tinkles and Melanie walks into the shop. Stan is busy with something and can't be here. We're meeting Mark and the new buyer for the walk-through today. For some reason, Melanie insists I be here. I guess if my name and position are in the contract as a contingency of the sale, I need to stick around. At the very least, I'll satisfy my curiosity as to who this new owner will be. Young? Old? Friendly? Stern? We'll see.

"Hi, Melanie. Can I get you a coffee?"

"I'd love one. But let's wait for Mark and the buyer."

"Does this buyer have a name?"

"Everyone does. Except, I guess, that musician named Prince who turned his name into a symbol. And then there was that football player that went by the number on his jersey."

I chuckle. I pick up a cup a customer left in the dirty dish area on the back counter.

"Do you feel like sharing his name?"

"The football player? I think it was Chad."

"No," I laugh. "The buyer."

"Oh. The buyer. No. I don't. I think he wants to introduce himself."

Great. A quirky owner. Who knows what this guy will want to change. He must be some sort of control freak to insist my name be in the contract, and then to not want anyone sharing his name.

The bell over the front door tinkles. I look up, and the cup in my hands clatters to the floor.

My mouth falls open. And then tears start streaming down my face.

Rene is here. In Cataloochee.

"Rene?" My voice is soft. Maybe I didn't even say his name out loud.

"Heather. Cher." He strides toward the back of the store.

I'm smiling like a fool. Rene is here. He's *here*.

I vaguely notice Melanie grabbing a broom to sweep the shards of the shattered cup I just dropped.

"I'm so sorry. I'll get that. Let me just ..."

"Don't you worry, dear. I've got this."

Rene stops only inches in front of me. He reaches out tentatively and cups my cheek, brushing his thumb gently across my skin.

"Rene. You're here. I didn't know you were coming to visit. What are you doing here? How long are you in town?" I'm rambling, and I don't ramble.

"I have business in town." Rene smiles and pulls me into his arms. "It is so good to see you, mon ange. I missed you so much. Tellement. You have no idea how my heart has ached ever since I returned to Avignon."

I dissolve into Rene's arms, feeling a rush of relief and a surge of warmth as he folds me into his embrace.

"Wait. What?" I lean back, placing my palm on Rene's chest and look up into his face. Oh, that face. "You have business here?"

"Oui." He pauses and smiles the mischievous, playful smile I have missed for forty-four days, not that I've been counting or anything.

Rene's smile grows brighter and then he says, "I am buying a coffee shop."

"You ..."

Melanie steps over toward us. "Heather, I'd like to introduce the new buyer. Rene DuBois. Rene, I think you have met Heather, the one you insisted we keep on as manager."

"You are the buyer? You?"

Rene looks down into my eyes. "Oui." He looks at Melanie. "Heather will be the manager for now."

"For now? Are you firing me at some point?"

I smile up at Rene, knowing whatever he has in mind, firing me is not a part of that plan. Will he buy Catty and run it from France? Is he moving here? I don't dare hope for that, but why else would he be buying this shop?

"Non, ma douce petite amie. When you are ready, I will make you a partner."

"A partner."

Rene smiles down at me, giving me the time I need to absorb everything. Questions rattle through my mind, but mostly, I'm overwhelmed by the rightness of his arms around me. This is where I belong. If I have to wait until Nate is out of school, I will. Then I will move to France if that's what it takes. I'm not going to live my whole life without this man and the way he fits me like no one ever has.

Melanie pats my shoulder. "I'm pretty sure the buyer has seen everything he needed to see. I'll show myself out. Why don't the two of you discuss the details in the office? I'm sure Simon can cover anything out here. I'll inform him before I leave."

Rene smiles warmly at Melanie. "Merci beaucoup, Melanie. I am grateful for your help and for keeping my secret. I owe you."

"Nonsense. Just seeing the two of you together is all the thanks I need. I've never seen this one smile quite as much as she is right now."

I blush, but I'm still smiling. You couldn't pay me to stop smiling.

Rene moves so his hand is on the small of my back. "Lead the way."

I walk ahead of him through the kitchen toward my office. "As you know, this is the kitchen. Soon to be *your* kitchen."

"Ah. I like the sound of that. My kitchen. My coffee shop. My girlfriend."

"Your girlfriend?"

"Oui. I am assuming. Should I ask? Maybe I should ask." He pauses us just in front of the office door. "Heather, mon cœur, would you be my girlfriend?"

"Oui. J'aimerais bien."

"What? You learned French?"

"No. Hardly. Only a few sayings. 'I would love to' is one of them."

"It is my favorite saying."

"Really?"

"Now it is."

Rene pulls me into a hug and then he leans in and kisses me with the kiss I've been waiting one and a half months for. And I kiss him with all the love and grief and relief swelling in my heart. My hands are in his hair. His are on my back, my arms, my face. We pull apart, only because I have questions that need answers.

"I need to know ..."

"Oui. Let me tell you."

His accent is stronger again. It had softened a little during his visit, but he sounds so much more French today. I love it. I love *him*. I nearly spit the words out, but I wait. We need to talk about everything with Catty before we go further and I dump out my ten year plan before he's even unpacked his bags.

"Have a seat," Rene says, pointing to my desk chair.

He leans back against the wall and smiles down at me. "A month ago, I had a serious talk with Pierre. I was so very miserable after my return to Avignon. I missed you so much. You will never know."

"I do know."

He smiles. "Maybe. You might know. My business was doing better than ever after I returned to France. My family and I spent time together on weekends. But I was so lonely, and my thoughts would always travel to you, and to Nate."

"You didn't call."

"I couldn't. I knew that would only make us both want what we couldn't have. I am right, non?"

"You are."

"Oui. So, I talked with Pierre and he said one thing that I could not stop repeating to myself."

"What did he say?"

"He told me I could tell you how I feel, or I could show you."

I'm quiet, smiling up at Rene because I still can't stop smiling. Even if this isn't leading where I hope it is, I am certain we have a future together.

"So, I asked myself day after day, 'How? How can I show mon cœur the love I feel for her?"

"Love?" I nearly choke on the word.

"Oui." Rene drops down so he is squatting in front of my chair. He reaches up and cups my cheeks. "Je t'aime, mon ange. I love you."

"I love you, too. Je t'aime aussi."

Rene dramatically clutches his hand over his heart. "Ah. You say it in French? You could not be more perfect."

"We both know I'm far from perfect."

"Hmmm." He looks dubious, but I know he knows. Thankfully, he knows my flaws—and he loves me despite them. *He loves me.* The truth of it sinks in just a little more and I smile even wider.

It could seem quick. It is quick. But we are older. We know our minds. We know our hearts. We have had the past six weeks to figure out whether what this is between us is real or just a passing fancy. We know now.

Rene stands up and leans against the wall again.

"Finally, I knew. I had to come here. Pierre also convinced me of this fact. He told me how much he misses

France. I thought I had to love America more than France to move here. It turns out I only had to love you more. And I love you so much more."

"I love you more too. I was going to move to France."

"What? When?"

"Well, not soon. I thought ... maybe after Nate graduates high school. In ten years, I could move there with you. I don't know how I could live in a foreign country when all I can say is croissant, and me too, and I love you, but it's a start."

"Oh, Cher. You would do that for me?"

"I would. I wish we had talked before you left—about our future."

"It wasn't time. We had only had three weeks together during my visit. Yes, we spent so many hours together. But we needed this time to prove to ourselves that we had not been dreaming—that what we felt was not passing or light. And I knew as soon as the plane touched down in Avignon that I had to be with you. It just took a few talks with my best friend and some arranging of my business to make it so."

"How did you buy Catty?"

"I have some properties—well, I had them—in Avignon and Provence. I sold a few. I called Mark after getting his number from Melanie. Then I made an offer. Mark told me, unfortunately at the time, the buyers were moving forward. He did assure me if the sale fell through, he would give me a call. So, two weeks ago, the buyers pulled out, and Mark called me. I spoke with Melanie and Stan and we began the paperwork."

"Including insisting this remain Cataloochee Mountain Coffee, and that I will stay on as the manager."

"Yes. Those were my terms, which they were happy to grant me."

A wave of nerves rolls through me as I ask the next question. "And you are going to run the business from America?"

"Oui. I am moving to Harvest Hollow. I will be with Pierre again, and see my nephew—or niece—when their baby is born. And I will be with you and Nate. When we decide we have been together long enough to be very serious, I will make you a partner in the business. You will be the co-owner of Cataloochee with me."

"I will pay you for that. I mean, I'll buy into my half of the business. I don't have all the money yet, but maybe we can work out a payment over time."

"If our assets are combined at that time, it will not matter." He winks at me.

Neither of us spells out that possibility any further. I'm pretty sure my smile says it all.

"Rene!" I jump up off my chair, unable to stay even a few feet away from him any longer. "Do Pierre and my sister know about this?"

"They do not. I wanted to talk to you first. You deserve to be the first to know."

"Where are you staying?"

"The Maple Tree Inn and Suites. My room at your sister's is now a nursery. My bed has been replaced with a crib."

I laugh.

"How long will you stay?"

"Until Christmas."

"Christmas?"

"Then I will visit my family in Avignon. Perhaps you and Nate will come with me. There are the Christmas Markets in France and other parts of Europe. I would love to take you."

"So you will only be here until Christmas?"

"Oui."

"And then you will move back to France?"

"No. Cher. No. I will be moving here for good now. I will only return to France to see my family at Christmas. And I hope you will come with me—to meet them, and to see my France."

"Oh! You're moving here? You are really moving here?" I sound like a giddy schoolgirl, or like Nate when I agree to a sleepover with his best friend. I don't care, though.

"I am. I will live here in Harvest Hollow. And as soon as I can, I will become a citizen of the United States, but I will remain a citizen of France as well."

"Oh, Rene! I can't believe you are doing this for me."

"And for me. I couldn't stand to be away from you. Also, for my family. They were getting so tired of seeing me moping around. And for Pierre. He was growing weary of my sad phone calls. So, you see, it is not only for you."

"Whatever you say."

I loop my arms around his neck and kiss him. He leans in and returns my kiss. This time we start off like race cars at the drop of the flag, but then our kiss slows, as if it dawns on us simultaneously that we have time now—all the time in the world. He is here. He is not leaving again. Rene runs his hand down my hair, then he pulls back and places a soft kiss on my forehead.

"This is the best close of a business deal I have ever had." His smile is roguish.

"Really? Your clients don't usually smother you in kisses?"

"Never. Only you, Cher. Only you."

EPILOGUE
RENE

If you live to be a hundred,
I want to live to be a hundred minus one day
so I never have to live without you.
~ A. A. Milne

Valentine's Day, One Year Later

"Mom! Come on! Rene is waiting down here," Nate shouts up to Heather.

I smile at him, and wink. I took a big risk letting him in on this secret. Nate is notorious for leaking confidences—usually at a loud volume, too. But I think we've all emphasized to him enough that tonight's surprise is one he simply can not let out of the bag, as they say here in North Carolina.

"Coming!" Heather shouts down. "In a minute!"

"Mom! I don't think you get what a minute means!"

I chuckle, but my laughter dies at the sight of Heather at the top of the stairs, and I wonder when I will ever get used to the way she makes me feel. I hope, never.

"Ouah. Si beau," I mutter, and then repeat loudly enough for her to hear the compliment.

"You always say that I'm so beautiful, even after a day of working at Catty."

"Because you are. I never say what I do not mean."

My girlfriend blushes.

"And you are wearing the red dress."

"That's what your note said: Wear the red dress. The one I bought you last year."

"For Valentine's Day."

"Which we used to hate, if you recall."

"I still hate it," Nate adds.

I smile at him. "Tell your mother how beautiful she looks."

"You look pretty good," Nate concedes.

"Is everyone ready?"

"I am." Nate tugs on his collar. "This tie is killing me. I don't know why I have to wear a tie. Grandma and Grandpa never made me wear a tie on Valentine's before."

"They said they are taking you somewhere special." I turn my head so only Nate can see me and I wink.

He winks back and it looks like he's trying to squeeze a lemon with his eyelid, but thankfully, Heather is grabbing her coat so she doesn't see him.

I step over to her and take the coat so she can slip into it.

"You look handsome, Rene."

"Thank you, Cher."

The three of us head out Heather's door, and we drive to drop Nate off with his grandparents on our way to Harvested. We have reservations at the same table where we ate last year for Valentine's Day.

"I'm having déjà vu." Heather teases me when we walk into the restaurant.

I sent her for a mani/pedi with Hannah earlier this afternoon, just like last year. This year, Hannah has a date too.

"That saying is French, déjà vu. Look at you, using even more French."

"Ha ha. Don't hold your breath for my mastery of your beautiful language. I may have already peaked."

"I am already so touched that you learned any words in French."

"You are too easy to impress." Heather beams up at me as we follow the hostess to our table.

We place our order. When the waiter walks away, I clasp Heather's hands in mine. "I love you, Cher. I am so grateful for this past year together."

"I love you too, Rene. Thank you for moving here, for buying the shop, for breaking through all my walls and teaching me I could love again."

"You never stopped loving, Cher. I did not teach you to love. You loved Nate and your sister and your parents and friends with the type of love few people show one another. You just needed to see that you could trust a man again."

"And you were that man? The one I needed to learn from?" She plays with me.

"Oui. And to think ..." I smile and wave a hand up and down my torso. "You almost missed out on all of this."

She laughs lightly, her eyes crinkling at the corners with amusement.

"Oh? What did I almost miss out on?"

"A man with an accent that should be broadcast over shopping mall speakers in place of the usual mind-numbing music."

"I did say that once, didn't I?"

"Yes. You did."

"And, a man who rubs your aching feet while listening to you chattering on about the insignificant details of your day." I raise my eyebrow and wink at her.

"Did you write down every compliment I ever paid you? Am I going to end up regretting saying nice things about you?"

"Maybe." I smile and lift her hand to my lips. I place a kiss on her knuckles and then return our enjoined hands to the table.

I didn't write these things down, but I remember every compliment she has ever paid me, word for word. What man wouldn't?

"Oh, and ... a man who makes your son break into regular fits of giggles."

"I did say that. And I'm not sure if that's a compliment or not."

"It is."

She laughs again. "Okay. It is. I love when the two of you get to laughing together. You disappear into your own shared, giddy little world. It's precious."

Then her face turns serious. "I was running scared when you came here last year. I don't know how you managed to bypass the bear traps and sinkholes and napalm bombs surrounding my previously annihilated heart. But I'm so glad you did."

I rub my thumb gently over her hand.

"You had every right to be wary of men. And you had every right to be skeptical about me. But I determined to help you overcome those things that held you back."

"You are a very determined man, Mister DuBois."

She looks at me through her eyelashes and I am tempted to ask for the check. But I have a plan to execute and her seductive glances will not derail me.

The door to the restaurant opens and Tasha and Pierre walk in, followed by Hannah and her date.

Heather turns her head to see what I'm looking at and sees them.

"Tasha!" Heather waves them over to our table. And then Heather sees her best friend. "Hannah?"

The four of them approach.

"What are you all doing here?" Heather asks.

"It is Valentine's Day, so I am taking my wife out for dinner," Pierre answers.

"Don't you two usually eat at home for special occasions? Especially now, with Lucas?"

My "nephew," Pierre's son, was born eight months ago. He's adorable. Nate is completely smitten with his baby cousin too. And I see Heather watching me when I hold Lucas. We are older than most people when they start dating, but not too old to become parents one day in the future. I have brought the idea up to Heather several times and she just smiles and tells me she wouldn't be totally opposed.

Hannah smiles at Heather. "We just came here for our date."

"Wow. I didn't realize everyone was coming to Harvested tonight. If it weren't Valentine's I'd suggest we get a big table and all sit together."

The four of our friends aren't even seated yet when the door to Harvested opens again and Nate walks in, followed by his grandparents. Heather's dad is carrying a sleeping Lucas in his car seat.

Heather's face scrunches up. "Mom? Dad? What are you doing here?"

I see my moment. Before anyone can clear up Heather's confusion, I set her hand back on the table and rise from my chair. She watches me walk around from my seat until I'm standing in front of her and then slowly dropping to one knee.

The expression on her face morphs from confusion to disbelief. And then her eyes gloss over with unshed tears and a wide smile appears on her face.

Our friends and family stand around us, quietly watching as I turn all my attention to the love of my life.

"Mon cœur. Je t'aime. I love you with my whole heart. You are my heart—mon cœur. I had never thought I would want to marry anyone. I fooled myself and everyone else. But when I set out to show you that love was possible, I fell for you. You captured my heart with your beauty, your generosity, your humor, and your strong spirit. And then, you gave me the most precious gift in return. You gave me your heart. I think you know I want to make a future with you. I am hoping you will be my wife, Heather. Will you marry me?"

"Oh, Rene." Heather's voice is soft and reverent.

"Oui, Cher."

"I would love to be your wife. Yes!"

I stand and take the ring out of my pocket and then I draw Heather up out of her chair and place the ring on her finger. I bend in and place a kiss on my fiancée's lips. She kisses me back, looping her hands behind my neck. The feel of her in my arms, the scent of my favorite perfume, the awareness of her answer all fuel me to forget our surroundings momentarily and deepen the kiss.

"Okay! Okay!" Nate says a little too loudly for the fancy restaurant setting. "Enough of the kissing."

Heather and I pull apart, laughing. Her eyes lock onto mine. I lean in and place another soft peck to her mouth.

Then I whisper, "Thank you, Cher. You have made me the happiest man in the world."

If you loved Rene and Heather's story, you can read their backstory in Pierre and Tasha's story in A Not So Fictional Fall.

Want more closed-door romcom from Savannah Scott? Check out all her books on Amazon.

Thank you for reading! I love sharing sweet and funny romance stories from my heart to yours!

Want to connect with Savannah Scott?

Be one of the readers who hears about new releases first, gets to participate in special giveaways, and sees sneak peeks into Savannah's writing ... join her weekly newsletter for all this and more.

Looking for a sweet group of readers who share life and books together? Join Savannah's Sweet Readers Facebook Group.

Or Follow Savannah on Instagram
And follow Savannah on Amazon for automatic notifications of new releases directly in your inbox.

All the Thanks ...

I want to thank **Gila Santos,** my copy editor. You are a sweet cheerleader and you see my blind spots. Thank you for believing in this story and me.

Tricia Anson. Goodness gracious. You are my friend, my proofreader, my personal assistant, the keeper of my sanity, and a gift in my life. I can't imagine what I'd do without you. Here's hoping I never have to find out.

Jessica Gobble, You are my bestie and my sister from another mister, Thank you for believing in me and praying over me all these years.

To my **Awesome "Shippers" and especially the CORE Team** who love me and my books so thoroughly. and to the **AMAZING Bookstagram Community.** I am so thankful for the way you support each book I write. Your sharing and celebrating of my work helps get these books out into the hands of other readers.

Thank you to **Mary Goad** for this cover. You just keep outdoing yourself!

Most of all, I want to thank **God** for calling me to be a storyteller and giving me the ability to make others smile and laugh.

Made in the USA
Las Vegas, NV
15 January 2024

84428675R00142